Just One More Affair

The Sterling Family
Book 5

NEW YORK TIMES BESTSELLING AUTHOR
Carly Phillips

JUST ONE MORE AFFAIR

Oops, she did it *again…*

A one-night stand with a billionaire.
A surprise pregnancy.
Can she trust his love?
Or is it the baby tying them together?

Charlotte Kendall never expected history to repeat itself after a one-night stand at a wedding. Especially since a past encounter left her co-parenting twin daughters she adores. Except this time, her baby daddy is a man she can't resist.

Billionaire Jared Sterling always gets what he wants—and he wants Charlotte Kendall. When he learns she's pregnant, he's all in. But Charlotte's past has taught this independent, single mom to guard her heart. She doubts Jared's motives and believes he's only invested for the baby.

Their chemistry is undeniable and Jared will do anything to convince Charlotte *she's* his endgame. But her life is complicated and when her brother's recklessness puts Charlotte in danger, Jared takes over, proving he's offering the love and stability she has always craved.

Now Charlotte must decide—will she keep running from the man who's offering her everything, or take a chance on love?

Chapter One

EVEN A SMALL Sterling family wedding was a lavish affair, Charlotte Kendall thought, looking around at the hotel ballroom where the reception was taking place.

Pink and white flowers twined around the ceiling with lilies dangling for effect. Each table had a luxurious burst of the same blush-colored flowers, a mix of roses, and other blooms surrounded by tea candles. The damask tablecloths were elegant. And the cocktail hour had four stations of different hot food choices along with servers walking around with various hors d'oeuvres.

The bride, Fallon Sterling, was Charlotte's daughters' new stepmother. Fallon had just married Noah Powers, the girls' dad. A man Charlotte had had a one-night stand with that resulted in a surprise pregnancy and a healthy co-parenting situation with their ten-year-old twins. She'd truly gotten lucky with Noah. They'd enjoyed one another once, but there had never been feelings between them and she was thrilled he'd found his soulmate in his younger wife.

As if he knew she'd been thinking of him, Noah

strode over and kissed her cheek. "Charlie, I can't tell you how much it means to Fallon and me that you came home for the wedding," he said, calling her by her nickname most people used.

"I wouldn't have missed it." But she appreciated him saying so. "Thank you for inviting me. Not everyone would understand our relationship."

"Fallon does, and that's what matters. We do a good job together with the girls."

She nodded. "And you've had the patience of a saint putting up with me following my dreams."

"I understand and if this is something you want to continue to do, I want you to know I'm okay with it."

She wrinkled her nose, having given her situation a lot of thought as the current dig was coming to an end. "As much as I loved the experience, I'm glad it's almost over. I miss the girls and having them full-time this week shows me how much I don't see on a day-to-day basis. They're changing and growing up and I want to be there."

He nodded. "Well, we'll work out a new arrangement and schedule when you're home for good."

"Hello, you two!" Fallon, who appeared to be floating with happiness, joined them and hooked her arm into Noah's. "Hi, Charlie. Thank you for flying in."

"Of course. And I need to thank you for all you do

for the girls."

Early on, Charlie had been worried about all the time Fallon had with the kids while she was away, but Fallon had proven herself wise for her years. She knew how to handle the twins and their precocious personalities, never tried to play mother, and deferred important decisions to Noah and Charlie. When Charlie moved back, she could see herself being Fallon's friend.

"I adore them and I'm glad we're making things work between us," Fallon said.

Charlie smiled. "Me too."

"Oh, this song!" Fallon exclaimed.

Charlie hadn't been paying attention to the music but when she focused, she heard the band had shifted to a slow song.

"I want to dance," Fallon said.

Noah laughed. "Guess that's my cue. Talk to you later, Charlie."

With a wave goodbye, Fallon led her new husband to the dance floor.

Given the choice between going to get a drink at the bar and watching the newlyweds dance, Charlie chose the former. She walked over to the luckily empty bar and picked up a glass of Champagne from several pre-poured flutes waiting on a tray.

She glanced around the room, her gaze falling on

Fallon's best friend, Brooke, who she'd met during one of her trips home. She was talking to her mother but she kept looking at Aiden Sterling, the journalist who wandered the world for stories. Charlie had often caught Aiden staring at Brooke, their gazes never meeting, and Charlie wondered what their story was.

"You look lost in thought. Is everything all right?" another of Fallon's brothers asked as he joined her.

Jared. Though Fallon had four siblings, Charlie had pegged this one as the best-looking of the group. The Sterling men were all extremely handsome, but Jared, with his piercing green eyes, stood out. His dark brown hair appeared as if he'd been running his hands through the strands but the tousled look was intentional, she knew from previous meetings. It suited him. Add in the tuxedo and he was sexy as hell. The wedding wasn't the first time they'd met. At a family gathering she'd been invited to, she'd been sitting next to him and he'd been utterly charming.

He cleared his throat and grinned, catching her staring.

She fought and lost the battle not to blush. Her cheeks heated with embarrassment. She also owed him an answer to his polite question.

"I'm fine. Just admiring the décor," she fibbed, taking a sip of the bubbly Champagne.

Turning to the server, he ordered a whiskey on the

rocks. "Dirty Dare brand, if you have it."

The woman in a white shirt and bow tie behind the bar nodded and poured him his drink.

He returned his focus to Charlie. "To meeting again." He touched his tumbler to her Champagne flute.

She smiled, warmed by the sentiment. "To meeting again."

A couple came up behind them and Jared grasped Charlie's elbow, leading her to a quiet space near a table that had emptied out, its occupants on the dance floor.

"So, how are you enjoying the wedding, Charlotte?" he asked, standing close.

She didn't mind. "Didn't I tell you my friends call me Charlie?"

"You did. I just happen to think Charlotte is a beautiful name and suits you." She caught the compliment, pleased he thought so. "But to be clear," he said, "I still consider you a friend."

"I'm very glad to hear it." Looking at this sexy, masculine specimen reminded her how long her dry spell had been. No sex since before she'd left for the dig almost two years ago. And maybe another six months before that. She definitely wouldn't mind being more than friends with Jared Sterling, at least for the night. "To answer your question, yes, I'm enjoying myself. Are you?" she asked.

His gaze raked her over, taking in her fitted lavender dress and stopping at the dip at her cleavage. "I am now," he said in a husky voice that sent a shiver of awareness tricking through her veins.

"Mommy! All the single ladies are lining up to catch the bouquet," her daughter, Dylan, said, her sister Dakota right alongside her.

The girls were dressed in pale pink dresses, their hair done in a thin mermaid braid holding back one side, looking adorable. They were growing up too fast. Not for the first time, Charlie wanted this dig to be over with so she didn't miss so much of their lives.

"Let's go try and catch it! We're all single!" Dakota raised her voice and tugged on Charlie's free hand.

Charlie met Jared's gaze and gave a little shake of her head. "I'm going to pass on this one, honey. Why don't you go stand with everyone and have fun?"

With a little luck, Fallon would toss high and a lucky single woman would catch the bouquet, not one of her ten-year-old girls.

"Let's go!" Dakota pulled her sister toward the dance floor, leaving Charlie alone with Jared once more.

"They're sweethearts," he said, a fondness in his voice she found truthful and not something someone said just to be nice.

She smiled. "Oh, don't let the dresses fool you. They can be trouble when they want to be."

He nodded. "But trouble can be good. Noah and Fallon wouldn't have met if they didn't think Fallon was you from behind."

His steady stare never left her face. His attention was all-consuming and she liked that about him. It left no doubt he was interested, too.

"Although… you must have cut your hair last year because Fallon's has always been much longer," he mused, telling her he was also observant.

"I cut it last time I came home from Egypt." She fluffed her shoulder-length bob. "It's easier to let air-dry in the desert."

"Well, I like the style. Frames your pretty face."

Her body heated even more, responding to the compliment. "Thank you."

She took a sip of the liquid, enjoying the bubbles as they went down. Charlie didn't drink often and especially not while on a dig, and this second glass had already gone to her head. She was nicely buzzed and happy talking to Jared.

"So, you aren't interested in the bouquet toss," he said. "I can't say I blame you. I have no intention of catching the garter. They're just silly superstitions."

"Traditions," Charlie said at the same time, and they grinned at the overlap.

"It's a wedding. All the lovey-dovey shit makes people think about having the same." He followed that proclamation by indulging in a large swallow of whiskey.

She nodded at the truth in his statement. "What about you? Are you looking for the same future Noah and Fallon have?"

He placed his drink on the table. "I've had no time to think about myself, to be honest. I work with my dad in Sterling Investments and he had a heart attack last year. We've all been on him to cut back on work, which leaves me carrying the bulk of the responsibility."

A family man, she mused, if not in the way she'd asked him. "I'm sorry about your father. But he seems healthy now."

He shrugged. "We hope. He's been caught with bad-for-him food and cigars." He paused in thought. "But enough about me and my family. What about you? You have the twins and your career, but is settling down in your future?"

At the question, the same one she'd thoughtlessly asked him, she felt herself close off inwardly. There wasn't an easy answer. Of course she'd want a man in her life. *If* she could trust one not to leave or let her down. If she could find someone who loved both her and her girls, who wouldn't forget his family like her father had after her mom passed away.

A sixteen-year-old girl needed her mother or at least a parent she could rely on, but her father hadn't been there. He'd buried himself in work and alcohol when home. All of which explained why finding what Fallon and Noah had wasn't likely. Her walls were too high.

"My career and the twins keep me busy enough," she murmured, deliberately vague. "I prefer to focus on now."

His brow wrinkled as he obviously pondered her answer and came to his own conclusions. "Speaking of now, the bouquet and garter toss are over." He tipped his head toward the center of the room. "Would you like to dance?"

His question drew her attention to the slow tempo of the music. "I'd love to," she said, placing her glass on the table.

She held out her hand. He took it and led her through the people standing and talking, weaving around the tables and winding up on the dance floor.

Soon, she was in his arms, moving seamlessly to the music. His hard body pressed deliciously against hers. And the masculine mix of tobacco and vanilla-scented cologne teased her senses and had her leaning in closer. His hand braced on her lower back as he led, and she found herself being seduced by everything that was Jared Sterling. One slow song led to another and she remained in his arms for a prolonged period of time.

"This might be too forward," he began. "But do you want to get out of here?"

Her heart skipped a beat. She was staying at this hotel until she left again tomorrow night. One more night and she'd be back in the sandy desert, living her dream but missing her girls, who were staying with Noah's parents in their hotel suite tonight and would remain with them while the newlyweds went on their honeymoon. She'd had the twins with her this past week and she'd be seeing them tomorrow at brunch for their goodbyes. Though she'd have loved to be with them one last night, she didn't want to upset them when they had to watch her pack to leave again.

"I have a room upstairs," she answered Jared at last.

"Then what are we waiting for?" His breath fanned her ear.

She let out a laugh at his impatient tone because she felt the same desire to be with him. "I need to say good night to Noah and Fallon, and to the kids."

"Let's each say our goodbyes and meet up by the ballroom door." His fingers squeezed her waist before releasing her.

Her body pulsed with anticipation as she walked up to Noah and Fallon, then the girls, explaining she had a slight headache and was going to go upstairs early. She wished the happy couple all her best, then hugged her girls and reminded them to be good for their grandparents.

Then she headed to the double doors where Jared was waiting. She wasn't sure if anyone saw them meet up and leave together but she'd deal with that if and when the time came.

They stepped into an elevator along with another couple she didn't know and she pushed the button to her floor. In silence they traveled upward, her body aware of Jared standing beside her. He'd taken off his jacket and hung it over one arm and was in the middle of removing his bow tie when the elevator car stopped and the couple stepped off.

"Damn, I hate these things," Jared muttered, attempting to undo the top button on his shirt next. "I wear a suit every day to work but a tuxedo strangles me."

She turned to face him and gently moved his hands. "Here. Let me." She undid the first button, then the second, realizing too late the intimacy in the act. Especially given their tight surroundings. She swallowed hard and patted the material over his chest with one hand. "There. All set," she said as a ding announced their arrival at her floor.

Jared snagged her hand in his and she led the way to her room.

Chapter Two

J ARED STOOD BESIDE Charlotte as she let them into her hotel room with her key card. The door shut with a click behind them. Her hips swayed as she walked inside and tossed her room card and purse onto the table in the outer room. She obviously had a suite to accommodate herself and the girls.

Turning, she met his gaze. Jared couldn't remember his last hookup but he had the definite feeling this would be one he wouldn't soon forget.

From the moment he'd met Charlotte this past year, he'd felt a connection. Talking to her had been easy and fun. They seemed to think alike and she was witty. Bright. And so fucking sexy she took his breath away. Without shame, he studied her, and from her high heels to the fitted light purple dress, she exuded sex appeal. Add in her tanned skin, beautiful face, luscious lips, and a shoulder-grazing haircut that showed her long, graceful neck and he was a goner.

"I'd offer you a drink but I don't have anything," she said with a high-pitched laugh that showed her apprehension.

"That's fine because I see something I want a lot

more." Determined to erase any nerves she might have, he stepped closer and slid a hand behind her neck, pulling her toward him.

When they were a breath apart, he waited, giving her one last chance to change her mind. Instead, she eased forward and their mouths met. He kissed her, parting her lips and taking his first taste. Her Champagne-tinged flavor along with her eager response did not disappoint. When she tangled her tongue with his, she triggered a primal response, one that had been building since they'd first met.

He spent long minutes devouring her mouth, tipping her head for better access and delving deeper. Tasting her felt like getting to know her better, more intimately. He ran his fingers through her hair, feeling the soft strands and tugging until she reacted with a soft moan.

His cock hardened and need raced through him, along with the desire to move things along. Sliding his lips over her cheek, along her jawline, and down her neck, he tasted her skin, breathing in her floral scent. She tipped her head, giving him better access, and he took his time, learning her likes and dislikes as he kissed, licked, and nipped at her skin.

Finally, he turned her around, kissing the back of her neck as he slid the zipper down her dress and peeled it off her shoulders. With a swipe of his hands, it fell to the floor, leaving her clad in only a matching pair of virginal-looking white lace underwear and bra. He already knew she wasn't naïve or a virgin, giving him permission to do so much more with her, and he loved it.

Pivoting her once again, he held her in front of him, admiring her until her chest flushed pink. "You're stunning," he said in gruff voice.

The light flush rose up and stained her cheeks.

"Thank you. Think you can even things up?" She reached out and began to unbutton the rest of his shirt, parting the sides and slipping it off his shoulders.

It caught on the cufflinks. He grinned and held out one hand for her to free his wrist, then the other. Then, he wasted no time undoing his pants and removing them along with his underwear and socks. His dick stood at attention, throbbing with need.

"Looks like we're uneven again," he said, his gaze on her soft mounds of flesh protruding over the white lace bra.

Her dark eyes never left his as she reached around her back and undid the clasp, letting it drop to the floor. The act revealed full breasts and dusky-colored nipples, and his mouth watered at the sight. She hooked her thumbs in her skimpy panties and pulled them off, tossing them onto the pile of discarded clothes.

"Even," she said, wrapping her arms around his neck and bringing their naked bodies in close contact.

His hard cock rubbed against her soft skin and he groaned at the feel of her feminine flesh.

"Play time's over," he stated, and lifted her fireman style over his shoulder, grinning as she shrieked and laughed at the same time.

Unable to resist, he gave her luscious ass a light slap. Instead of yelling in outrage, her silence was followed by a long, pleasure-filled moan.

He picked up his pace and deposited her on the mattress in the center of the bed. Placing one knee beside her, he intended to join her, when he paused, reality hitting him.

"Shit. We need protection," he said, grinding his teeth at the thought of not feeling her wet, tight heat around his.

"I have an IUD," she said, their gazes meeting. "And I had every test under the sun before I left for the dig. There's been no one since."

"Good to know," he said, his voice tinged with the same relief flowing through him. When it came to this woman, he was discovering he had a caveman side. One that wanted everything she was willing to give. As much as she'd let him explore and get to know her better, he was all in.

Wait.

What?

This is a one-night stand, he reminded himself. The truth was, he had no time for a relationship and even if he did, she lived across continents. Their worlds had crossed for this short period of time only. Besides, when he was younger he'd tried dating and not one woman had the patience for the hours he put in at work.

A small voice asked if that was because maybe he'd never found the right woman. No. He shook his head and caught her curious expression, her nose crinkling as she obviously waited for him to give his status on protection.

Instead, he'd gotten lost in crazy daydreams.

He cleared his throat and his mind of anything other than the current situation. "After my father's heart attack, common sense made me get a physical. The whole nine yards," he told her. "I'm clean. And yeah. As I said, I have no time for a social life." It'd been longer than he cared to admit since the last time he'd had sex with any woman.

Charlotte's eyes darkened at his words. "So we can still…?"

The question trailed off and knowing what she'd been thinking, he nodded. "We can. Which means the time for talking is over." Grasping his erection, he pumped with his hand, his palm grazing from root to tip, and he grit his teeth at the desire coursing through him.

Joining her on the bed, he leveraged his body over hers, kissing her once more. After taking time with her mouth, he moved down her body, licking, kissing, and tasting until he reached her center, swiping his tongue through her pussy, finding her wet for him. His dick gave a hard pulse of need and at the same time he exhaled a low groan, she let out a shuddering moan. He could play some more but they were both on the edge.

He kissed her belly once, then twice, before sitting up, gripping his cock and lining himself up at her entrance. Their eyes met as he pushed inside her for the first time. Pumping his hips in short bursts, he eased his way into her, making sure she was slick and ready.

She was wet with need but he was thick and she needed priming. He took his time, watching her face, making him aware of her increasing pleasure. Three more passes in and he bottomed out deep, her body accepting all of him.

"Jared, I feel you everywhere," she murmured, squeezing her core muscles tighter around him.

"That's the point." Unable to hold back, he lifted his hips and slammed deep once more.

"Oh God!" Her eyes glittered with desire and he

complied, slamming into her, pressing her deeper into the mattress.

Her breath came in short pants and he feared he'd come too quickly.

"*More.*" She continued to beg for him to thrust harder and deeper and he was only too happy to oblige.

He had another trick up his sleeve and he slid his hand between them, stroking her clit back and forth until she lost any sense of rhythm.

"I'm so close." Her body trembled beneath him, her inner walls clasping him harder.

"Then let go." He pinched her clit between his thumb and forefinger and she stiffened, then began to shift her hips against his. She let go, crying out and riding out a climax that seemed to last for a gloriously long time as he held on, determined not to follow her over just yet.

He slid out, flipped her over, and pulled her up on her hands and knees. Repositioning himself, he slid back in, the new angle causing her to grip him tighter and from the scream she let out, he'd hit a new spot inside her. One that made her wild and she threw her head back, meeting him as he thrust in and out, so fucking close.

Recalling what she'd enjoyed, he rubbed a hand over one ass cheek and gave her a light slap, then massaged the area until she let out a whimper.

"I didn't know that could feel good," she admitted.

He couldn't say this was normally his thing, but with Charlotte, he wanted to experience her locking his cock in a tight vise, trusting him not to hurt her, but to provide all the pleasure she deserved.

He slapped the other cheek.

"Oh God, yes."

He then thrust into her, slamming hard as he made sure to hit the sweet spot inside her, over and over until she cried out his name. Knowing she was mid-climax, he let go, coming until he thought he'd blacked out.

They collapsed on the bed and he pulled out, rolling to the side so as not to crush her. Once he caught his breath, he glanced over. She lay on her stomach, face to the side, breathing heavily.

"You okay?" he asked, sliding her hair off her cheek so she could breathe more easily.

"You broke me," she said, laughing.

"In a good way, I hope."

"The best way possible." She shifted to the side and met his gaze. "Despite what it may seem like given the situation with the twins, I don't do this often." She gestured between them with one hand.

"I never thought you did."

She offered him a sweet smile. "I meant to say, I

don't do this often, nor do I plan to, but I can guarantee, this was the best time ever."

"You're good at giving compliments." He leaned over and kissed her cheek. "Be right back."

He slid out of bed and walked naked to the bathroom where he washed up, found an extra hand towel, wet it with warm water, and returned to find Charlotte where he'd left her.

He sat on the bed and cleaned her gently as she watched him, her gaze soft. "Thank you, Jared."

He smiled, liking how his name sounded on her lips. "You're welcome. Now, get some sleep." He rose to his feet, planning to return the towel to the bathroom.

"Are you leaving?" she asked, sounding disappointed.

He couldn't contain the pleasure he felt at her reaction. "Not if you don't want me to."

She shook her head. "I don't."

So he put the towel in the bathroom, climbed into bed, and pulled Charlotte into his arms.

UNSURE HOW LONG he'd slept, Jared woke to a warm body wrapped around his. This was a rare to never happens occurrence and he knew immediately where he was and hoped for a morning quickie before he had to say goodbye to Charlotte.

A flash of disappointment hit him at the realization this couldn't be anything more than it was.

"Morning," she said, and he rolled to his side, facing her.

Her chocolate-colored eyes were half-mast, her hair messy, and she still looked beautiful to him. "Good morning. Did I wake you?" He'd tried not to move or jostle her.

She shook her head. "My internal clock is pretty strong. I've been waking up around seven with the girls. What time is it?"

He glanced at the clock on the nightstand beside her and grinned. "Seven o'clock."

She stretched her arms over her head and her breasts popped out from beneath the blanket. Blushing, she grabbed the covers and pulled them back up. "Oops."

"Didn't bother me," he said with a chuckle. Despite wanting her again—how could he not?—he had the sudden urge to also know more about her. "Are you ready to go back to your dig?" he asked her, curious about her lifestyle.

She paused, wrinkling her nose as she thought. "I guess so, but when I'm there I miss home. But we still have work to finish." She sounded more resigned than excited.

"Is it hard to leave the girls?" He couldn't imagine just taking off to another country for a couple of years if his kids were here.

"Very hard. But there's a part of me that's following my mother's dream. *Our* dream," she clarified.

"How so?"

She pulled in a deep breath and exhaled before beginning an explanation. "Mom, her name was Kylie, was a curator at a museum. She loved ancient artifacts and history, and passed that love on to me. From the time I was young, she used to take me with her to work. My older brother stayed with the babysitter but I was a bookworm, so I never minded being at the museum. I used to ask her so many questions." Her lips tilted upward at the memory.

"You sound like Dakota and her never-ending facts."

Charlotte laughed. "She's more precocious than I ever was. I was more serious. But I couldn't get enough of paleontology and history and my mother always indulged me with patient answers."

"You two were close." It wasn't difficult to figure that out.

Smiling, she nodded. "I miss her."

"What happened?"

Charlotte swallowed hard. "She died from cancer when I was sixteen."

He reached for her hand. "I'm so sorry."

Given his age when his own mother passed away, murdered by one of his father's clients when he was thirteen, he knew how hard this must have been on her. It didn't seem like the right time to bring up his past. He was focused on hers.

"Thank you," she murmured. "Mom had always wanted to go on a dig for ancient artifacts, but she became pregnant with my brother. And let's just say my father was nothing like Noah."

Jared appreciated the insight she was giving him into her life. "Noah is an exceptional parent," he said. "And he's understanding when it comes to you and your work. You two have an unusual but very fortunate agreement about raising the kids."

She nodded. "I'm forever grateful to him. Mom and I used to talk about trying to go on a dig together after I graduated college but... obviously, it never happened and I was determined to do it on my own. I just never expected this dig to keep getting extended as often as it has."

They lay in silence, her story settling inside him as he thought about their shared loss and how much she'd loved her mother. "Thank you for telling me," he said.

"I don't mind talking about Mom. It makes me feel close to her, as does being on the dig. But I have a lot to make up to Dylan and Dakota."

Her love for the kids was obvious. "You're setting a good example for them about being true to themselves."

"I appreciate you saying that. I fight the guilt daily." She shook her head, as if ridding her mind of unhappy thoughts. "Now, how about some *us* time before I have to meet the girls for breakfast?"

She didn't have to ask him twice. He reached out and pulled her into his arms, his lips coming down on hers when her phone rang from her nightstand. She must have gotten up for it during the night.

With a groan, she rolled over and answered the call. By the time she hung up, he knew from the gist of the conversation the girls wanted to come see her and their time together was over.

Chapter Three

Two Months Later

CHARLIE PACKED THE last of her things and zipped her large duffel bag closed. She looked around her trailer to make sure she hadn't accidentally left anything behind.

Nope.

Even the picture of the twins that had sat on the table beside the bed was safely tucked away for the trip home.

Her flight was one day away, as they had today for their drive back to civilization. A one-night stay in a hotel tonight, a flight to New York tomorrow, and she'd settle into another hotel and see her girls. Then, she'd have to find herself an apartment and a job. But the twins were her priority, along with her newly discovered *situation*.

Though Noah lived in a much more exclusive area than she could afford, there were neighborhoods nearby she might be able to manage. Prior to the dig, she'd worked for a museum and though she hadn't wanted to take money from Noah, he'd insisted on contributing for the girls, which had enabled her to compile a small savings. She'd refused to continue to take from him while she was away but he insisted on resuming his payments now that she was home. As long as she got a good-paying job, she'd be fine.

"Knock, knock!" Professor Jerome Wilson said, accompanying his rap on her open door. Jerome had led the dig and had been the person who hired her in the first place.

"Come in!"

He was nearing sixty, his hair a silvery gray, and he was a nice-looking man. He also had a wife at home who was even more understanding than Noah since he went from one excursion to the next.

"You're all set to leave, I see," he said, taking in her closed duffel.

"I'm ready to be home."

"I can understand how much you miss your girls. But I have a proposition for you, and it would give you six months before you have to leave again."

Leave again? Not happening, she thought. "Jerome, as much as I appreciate whatever it is you're going to offer, there is nothing that can convince me to leave my daughters again. This dig was the opportunity of a lifetime for me. We've excavated and catalogued artifacts that would never have been seen otherwise and I loved the excursion. But I'm done."

Disappointment flashed across his face, the twinkle in his eyes dimming. "What if I told you I'm heading a group going to Alexandria to search for Alexander the Great's tomb?"

She stared in disbelief. "Not only has that been considered lost but people have searched for years. Calliope Limneos-Papakosta has been there for years."

"And I'd like to meet up with her. Aren't you interested?"

She closed her eyes and gave the opportunity serious thought. Not even a hint of desire. Would she be fascinated to read about it? Of course. But she was tired and would love to find a job like her mother had, and like she'd had before her dig, in a New York City museum.

"I'm sorry, but my main title is going to be mommy from now on. I'll find a job and I have your letter of reference to help me." She smiled, but he didn't return the gesture.

He shook his head, his displeasure clear. "I'm quite disappointed."

She raised and lowered her shoulders. "I have to do what is right for me." She wouldn't apologize for her decisions.

"Well, I respect your choice. I'll see you when our ride arrives." He tipped his head and walked out of the trailer.

She stepped toward the entrance and shut the door, locking it behind him. Sitting down on the bed, she dug into her backpack carry-on and grabbed the inside zipper, pulling out the plastic bag holding the pregnancy test she'd taken this morning.

Luckily for her, Layla, her closest friend and confidante on this trip, had joined one of their guides and gone to the nearest town for personal supplies and necessities. She'd picked up the test and Charlie trusted her to keep her request private.

She glanced at the stick in her hand and the two vibrant pink lines staring back at her. If the news weren't so serious she'd have to think it was a joke. Who got pregnant by one-night stands twice in one lifetime?

She'd had her IUD put in after giving birth to the girls, and though she planned on having it removed and a new one put in once she was home, she thought for certain hers was still good.

She sighed. Despite not having had much time to adjust to the news, she wasn't as panicked as she'd been with Noah. Back then, she'd barely had a grasp on her life. Now she was turning thirty soon, had a degree and experience that would qualify her for a well-paying job, and she was even excited to have another baby.

As for Jared? Her stomach flipped at the thought

of him. Since her return from the wedding, she'd thought of him almost daily. She'd also had the fleeting thought it hadn't been smart to sleep with someone she'd surely see at family events when she came home.

Now, she wondered how he'd take the news.

AS PER USUAL, Jared worked past five. He was CFO and his father was CEO. Though Jared was used to the long hours, tonight he was damned tired. Deciding to pack it up early—for him—he gathered some paperwork and walked to his father's office, planning to leave the information for him to see in the morning.

The lights were on beneath the door, taking Jared by surprise. Another example of his father ignoring the strict rules given to him by the doctor.

Jared shook his head in frustration. He wanted his dad around for a long time, not taking stupid risks with his health. Jared had already restructured both his life and the company to accommodate his father. He'd taken on the bulk of Alex's work and had promoted Brooklyn Snyder, the daughter of their housekeeper and now his father's girlfriend, not to mention his sister Fallon's best friend, to an executive position. They worked closely together and made a good business team. The only one not cooperating was his dad.

Gritting his teeth, he knocked once and walked into the office. His father sat in his leather chair watching a finance channel on the wall-mounted television screen, a lit cigar sitting on an ashtray.

Pissed, Jared stormed over, picked up the cigar, and snubbed it out. "Do you have a death wish?" he asked his father. "Working late, smoking... let me guess. You'll shower here?" He pointed at the full bathroom in his father's office. "And Lizzie won't know the difference?"

"She's out with her friends," he grumbled. "I'll be home and showered before she even comes back from dinner. I was just getting ready to leave."

Jared shook his head. "Not the point and you know it. Explain your behavior to me because I don't understand. We've done everything we can to remove the stress from your life. All you need to do is work less hours, moderate your diet, and stop smoking those damned cigars."

His father's face turned from stoic to sad, his mouth turning downward in a frown. "You don't know what it's like getting older. Being told what I can and cannot do. Even Lizzie looks at me differently. What if I slow down and she wants a younger man? The kind of man I was before the heart attack?"

With a sigh, Jared lowered himself into the seat across from his dad's mahogany desk. A photo of his yacht covered one wall and a family portrait was on another. If Alex wanted more time with either, he needed to behave.

"Dad, I can't pretend to understand how you're feeling, but there are a few things I know for a fact. One is that Lizzie loves *you*. It doesn't matter to her what you can or can't do. You're still the same man she fell for. And two, your kids want you around for the foreseeable future." He leaned forward in his seat, hands clasped in front of him. "We love you, Dad. Don't you want to be there when Fallon has the baby?"

"Of course I do!" he said loudly, slamming a hand on the desk.

Tough love was all Jared had left. "Then get your act together!" Bracing his arms on the chair, Jared pushed himself to his feet. "Now, unlike you, I'm leaving early. I'm wiped out from getting in at seven a.m. You should do the same."

"I'll meet you by the elevators and we can go down together," his dad said. "Changing the subject, will you be at the get-together at the house on Saturday? Since Aiden is home on a break, I'm looking forward to having all my kids together under one roof."

Jared's youngest sibling was a traveling reporter,

breaking stories around the world, but he'd confided that the wandering lifestyle was getting old. It made Jared wonder what, if anything, his change of heart had to do with Brooklyn. While growing up as teens, Brooke, as they all called her, had been close with his brother. Until they weren't. And neither ever spoke of what had changed.

"I'll be there, Dad."

"Great! The twins invited their mother. Should be interesting hearing about her exploits and what they found during her dig."

He stood up straighter. "Charlotte is in town?" He hadn't heard anything about her from Fallon or Noah and had known better than to ask. At the sound of her name, his heart began a steady thump and his dick... well, let's just say he needed to excuse himself before his father noticed his reaction.

"She wrapped up her excursion and is staying in a hotel until she finds a place to live. The girls want to be with her constantly, so she's invited."

"Sounds good," he said, playing off the information as if it meant nothing to him. "I need to go to my office and get my things. Meet you by the elevator." He strode out of the office and walked to his, his thoughts on Charlotte and their night together.

Since he was alone, he adjusted his cock and began to pack up for the night. Though he hadn't heard from her since she'd left—not that he'd tried to reach her either—she'd been on his mind. Constantly. He hadn't dated often before Charlotte, having given up after trying when he was younger and working to learn the business. After Charlotte? He'd had no interest. Not even in a casual hookup to take the edge off.

She'd been special. He might not have been looking for anything more than a one-night stand, but they'd gotten along so well and the sex had been incredible. Better than anything he'd experienced before, probably due to their level of comfort with one another and the strength of the attraction. Though sleeping with someone so connected to his family hadn't been his brightest idea, he still couldn't wait to see her again.

For the first time in a long time, he had something to look forward to.

Chapter Four

CHARLIE HAD BEEN back in New York City for the last two weeks. She'd spent the time acclimating to the time change, to the hotel she was living in until she found an apartment she liked and could afford, sending out résumés and spending time with her girls.

She drove to Jared and Fallon's parents' house in the suburbs, the kids seat-belted into the back of her rental car, chatting away.

"Mommy? When you move can we get a dog?" Dakota asked.

"I want a cat," Dylan said.

"Hmm. Did you know a pope decided cats were bad and had them all killed? And that's why the bubonic plague spread! 'Cause there were no cats to catch the rats. Maybe we should get a cat to keep the rats away," Dakota jumped in with one of her *fun* facts.

Oh, her smart, wise-ass child, Charlie thought, doing her best not to laugh at Dakota because she found her so darned cute.

"No, sweetheart, that's a myth." It was more complicated than that but she didn't feel like getting into it now. Not when her stomach was twisting with nerves because she was going to have to face Jared soon.

"Then I still want a dog." Charlie glanced in the mirror in time to see Dakota fold her arms across her chest, and she had no doubt Dylan was gearing up for the cat argument.

"Mommy!" Dylan wailed.

And there it was.

"Girls, we're at Grandpa's house. Can we stop arguing and just enjoy the day? There won't be any animals in the near future because you two are in school all day and I, fingers crossed, will have a full-time job."

She pulled into the driveway and parked the car. The girls unbuckled their seat belts and opened their doors, running for what was sure to be the unlocked front door.

Charlie took the time alone to gather herself. Seeing Jared again would be trying enough, their night together still fresh in her mind, but knowing she was pregnant with his child made the upcoming encounter even harder. Although she knew she needed to tell him, this wasn't the time or the place. An excuse? Maybe. But she didn't know him that well.

She already knew he wasn't thinking about a family at this point in his life—his words to her at the wedding. What if he was upset with her? She'd seen a doctor and knew her IUD was old and had probably failed. Despite the fact that it took two to make a baby, she felt responsible for this unplanned pregnancy since she'd assured him she was protected.

And what were the chances he'd be another Noah and take the news as a shock, but once he wrapped his head around it, in stride? What if he blamed her for saddling him with a kid? She was more than capable of being a single mom without his help but the family connection made things tricky.

Blowing out a breath, she picked up her bag, and the tray of cookies she'd bought at a bakery before leaving the city, then exited the car. She strode up the walkway and let herself into the house, as directed by Fallon. The sheer scale of the place overwhelmed her, as did the wealth she knew they had. Though not ostentatious, the structure was massive, with a gatehouse and pool in the back. It was a far cry from how she'd grown up in a small, run-down house her father rarely kept up.

Noise sounded from the rear of the house and Charlie headed in that direction, walking into a massive family room filled with people. Before she could say hello to anyone, and the entire family appeared to be there, the girls ran up to her.

"Lizzie made pigs in a blanket!" Dylan said. "Want some?"

"Did you know pigs eat humans?" Dakota asked.

At the statement, Dylan's eyes filled with tears. "Mommy, is that true?"

She glanced at her other daughter. "Dakota, that's enough," she said, before turning to Dylan. "Did Wilbur eat Charlotte?" she asked.

Dylan sniffed. "No."

"Well then. Bring me a hot dog. We can each have one."

"Okay!"

"Whew. Subject changed," she said aloud.

Laughter followed that statement and she found herself saying hello to everyone, hugging some she'd met at the wedding, and overall feeling welcome, for which she was grateful.

She turned and bumped into the one person she hadn't said hi to yet. "Jared."

"Hello, Charlotte."

He stood close, his nearness a jolt to her system. He smelled familiar and sexy. It was all she could do not to lean into him, inhale the same arousing, masculine scent he'd had on at the wedding.

Catching herself, she smiled at him. "Hi. How have you been?"

"Busy with work and keeping my father in line. So basically, the usual," he said, his gaze raking her over, studying her and taking her in, and her body heated

40

with awareness. "I heard you're back for good."

"Someone has been talking," she mused. *Or has he been inquiring about me?* she wondered but wouldn't ask. "I came home a couple of weeks ago and I'm staying in a hotel until I can find a place to move. I want to be near Noah so the back-and-forth with the twins is easy on us both."

"That makes sense," he said.

"Hi, both of you," Fallon said, joining them, Noah by her side.

"Hi." She turned to Fallon. "Thanks for inviting me. The girls were so happy and I appreciate it."

"My pleasure. So, I couldn't help but overhear you talking about needing a place to live. I was going to discuss this with you anyway, so here goes. Especially with both of you here," she said.

Noah put an arm around Fallon's shoulder. "What are you thinking?" he asked his wife.

"Just that Jared owns three apartment buildings near where you live." Fallon met her brother's gaze. "Do you have any open ones? The building where you live is the closest."

And Charlie was sure it was the most expensive.

Jared raised an eyebrow. "Actually, I think there is. I'll check with my manager."

"Oh, that's not necessary. I'm sure it's out of my budget," she said, feeling heat rise to her cheeks.

Noah stepped over to her. "Can we talk?"

"Umm, sure." She followed him to a private spot in the hall.

Once they were alone, he began to speak. "Listen, I know you want to be independent and you don't want to take more from me than I insist for the girls. But the fact is, you being nearby benefits everyone."

"I know but—"

He shook his head. "No buts. Having a safe place to live will make me feel better, and not just when the twins sleep over. If we'd married and divorced, you'd be entitled to alimony. Just because we co-parent doesn't mean I can't help out."

She closed her eyes, hating that he was right. She'd rather live somewhere safe for the girls' sake, not to mention her own. The places she'd seen listed were far from ideal. Small space, not comfortable for her daughters. Even the neighborhoods bordered areas where she wouldn't want the kids playing outside.

"Okay, but I won't take advantage. I have savings and I know one of my résumés will pan out. I have solid experience."

He smiled. "I'm not worried about you finding a good job. You're excellent at what you do."

"Thank you, Noah. You've always been more than generous. I hate feeling like a burden. The girls are your concern, I shouldn't have to be."

He shook his head. "You aren't a burden. Put that out of your head and let's go enjoy the day."

She nodded and followed him out of the hallway to find Jared had waited for her.

"Hungry?" he asked.

"Not really."

He grasped her elbow. "Then let's sit down and discuss apartments."

They wound their way through family, stopping to talk to various people. At least twenty minutes passed until they finally settled on a sofa to have their discussion.

"So, tell me what you're looking for. How many bedrooms, bathrooms, etc.?"

Knowing the girls were growing up and Noah would want them to have the comfort with her that they had at home, and aware she needed a room for the baby, she forced herself to scale up. "Three bedrooms, enough for the girls to move into their own rooms, though right now they want to be together. And two full bathrooms." She couldn't imagine sharing one during the upcoming tween years.

She didn't deny she needed a nice place to live, but did it have to be the building where Jared lived? Knowing he was so close would wreak havoc on her senses. Memories of their night together constantly surfaced both during the day and when she tossed and turned at night, trying to sleep.

If she lived near him, she'd be wondering about running into him and be tempted to stop in and say hello. Not to mention, she still had to tell him about the baby and either he'd be angry or he'd want her closer. Given how she valued her independence, she couldn't let him take over.

"Actually, make that four bedrooms." She swallowed hard. "I need a place to work from home." In reality, she needed a nursery, but she didn't plan on giving him an explanation for that yet. Of course she needed Noah's help. No way could she afford even a two-bedroom in a nice area of Manhattan on her own.

He nodded. "Okay then. When are you free to check out a couple of places in my buildings?"

She bit down on her lower lip. Knowing they were going to have to spend prolonged time together, she decided to get it over with. "How's tomorrow?"

"Ten a.m.?"

She nodded.

"Give me your phone." Handing it to him, she watched as he typed his cell into her keypad and hit send. "Now we have each other's numbers. Text me if you need anything," he said.

Overwhelmed, she managed a smile. "I will."

The rest of the day passed and Charlie pushed her problems to the back of her mind, enjoying watching her children interact with their family, eat Lizzie's cake like little animals, and helping them clean up their chocolate-covered faces. All the things she'd missed while away.

When the girls asked if they could sleep with her at the hotel, Noah agreed.

She gathered their things, because Grandpa and Lizzie always gave gifts, said their goodbyes, and headed out the door, feeling the heat of Jared's stare as she left.

JARED WATCHED CHARLOTTE and the girls leave. The rest of the family was in the kitchen and Jared had escaped into the family room for a breather; time to think and wonder what it was about Charlotte that drew him in. She needed somewhere to live? He wanted to make sure she had one. A safe place for her and the girls. Usually, he was preoccupied with work. Instead, he was taking the morning off tomorrow to show her apartments.

"Hey." Aiden came up beside him and settled in on the sofa.

"Hey, yourself. So how's it feel to be back?"

Though Aiden had stayed in New York for a month after their father's heart attack, he'd taken off again for a job abroad covering a hostage release in the Middle East. He'd remained in the region afterward instead of returning. Until now.

"Better than I thought it would. Guess I needed the normalcy of home." Aiden kicked his feet out in front of him and leaned back against the cushion. "Did I tell you I was a car behind an IED explosion?" he asked as casually as he'd talk about the weather.

"What the fuck?" Jared asked. Shock and fear for what might have happened to his brother rolled through him. "This is how you tell me?"

Aiden shrugged, then rubbed his hand behind his neck, the only indication that the incident had disturbed him. His brother had nerves of steel. "I didn't want you to worry if you couldn't see I was in one piece."

Jared closed his eyes and groaned. "You don't make it easy," he muttered. "Thank God you're okay."

"Just don't tell Dad." Aiden's tone was serious, and Jared agreed. No need to add to their father's stress.

"I won't. Keep your ass out of danger?" Jared asked his brother.

Aiden nodded and let out a shaky laugh. "I'll consider it."

Jared knew that was as much of a promise Aiden would make.

"So, what's with you and Charlie?" Aiden asked, changing the subject. "I saw you huddled together talking to her earlier."

"Everyone else talked to her too." Realizing his answer sounded defensive, he gave his brother more information. "Fallon asked if I'd show her the empty apartments in my buildings since she's looking for a place to live."

"And that's why I caught you staring at her ass and giving her puppy dog eyes like a teenager?" Aiden grinned.

"Shut the fuck up. I was not mooning. I was… admiring."

Aiden tipped his head to the side, studying him. "Oh yeah? At Fallon's wedding, too? I saw you two dancing."

"What are you? My babysitter? Besides, it's been two months since the wedding and you're just mentioning you saw us now?"

"I haven't been here to do it," he said.

"Maybe it's time you were."

Of all his brothers, Jared was the closest to Aiden, which was why his sibling's need to travel was most difficult on Jared. He not only missed talking to him but he hated not being able to reach him at will. Between time differences and how busy they both were, long conversations were impossible.

"Maybe it is."

Jared blinked, stunned at the answer, but before he could reply, Aiden spoke again. "Now, about Charlie…"

"I call her Charlotte."

Aiden smirked. "So make a move."

Jared sighed. "My life doesn't lend itself to a relationship. The business and Dad keep me busy enough."

"Not too busy to show her apartments." He leaned forward in his seat. "Isn't Brooke helping out at the office? You promoted her, right?"

"A well-deserved, overdue promotion. Between the two of us we're running things, but it isn't fair of me to dump extra work on her because I want a social life."

Aiden laughed. "At least you admit you want one. I'd say that's a start."

Jared grudgingly agreed with a grunt, then changed the subject. "Now, speaking of personal lives, let's talk about Brooke."

"Let's not." Aiden pushed himself up from his seat.

Jared knew there was intense history between them. He just didn't know everything and he had a feeling she was part of what kept Aiden away. The other being their mother's murder and survivor's guilt.

Both Aiden and Jared had been away at summer camp and there was nothing either could have done. In truth, there was nothing they could have changed had they been home, either.

Was that guilt what drove Jared to work so hard and protect his father at the expense of any kind of life for himself? Perhaps. But he had a feeling Charlotte Kendall was about to change all that. For better or worse remained to be seen.

Chapter Five

THE NEXT MORNING came all too soon. The sound of the girls' chatter lightened Charlie's mood and put into perspective the need to meet with Jared and find an apartment. It had taken her hours to fall asleep last night, and she lay awake listening to them giggling in the double bed next to hers.

Once they were dressed, she took the twins down to the hotel restaurant for breakfast where Fallon would pick them up. It was summertime, so they were off from school and Fallon had hired an assistant manager at the gallery to help her out, giving her more time when the baby arrived. She was always willing to help with the girls.

"Want some of my eggs?" Dylan asked, sticking her fork into the yellow scrambled mass and holding it out for Charlie.

She shook her head and quickly looked away, feeling queasy.

Overall, she'd had an easier time with nausea this pregnancy than she'd had with the girls because... twins, so she attributed today's bout to nerves. She had to tell Jared he was going to be a father. Explaining to her daughters could wait, though.

She took a sip of herbal tea, wishing it was a hard dose of caffeine instead.

"Fallon's here!" Dakota said, rising from her seat.

"Wait until she comes to you." Charlie added a tip and signed the bill to her room before turning to see Fallon striding toward them.

She had her own look, favoring long skirts and eclectic tops, whereas Charlie preferred leggings, flowing floral blouses or men's-styled shirts, and when home, fitted gym clothes, which would be interesting when she began to show. She'd been so huge with the twins she'd had to wear loose clothing.

"Morning, Fallon." Charlie rose from her seat. "I appreciate you taking them while I look at apartments. The day would bore them to tears."

Fallon chuckled. "I understand. Are you ready, girls?"

They gathered their things. "Fallon, Mommy's taking us to the Museum of Natural History this week. Want to come?"

Fallon glanced at Charlie and shook her head. "You need time with them."

"You're more than welcome. You know that."

"Next time." Turning to the girls, Fallon said, "I'll come on another trip. Ready? I want to stop at the gallery and show you some new art."

"Yay!" they chimed in unison.

"Give me a hug," Charlie said. The girls took turns with big hugs and *I love yous*, something Charlie had desperately missed while away. FaceTime wasn't the same.

They walked off with Fallon, leaving Charlie alone with a few minutes to herself before she had to leave to meet up with Jared. He'd texted her the address for the first building and true enough, it was close to Noah's.

She took the subway to the nearest station and walked the rest of the way. The sun shone down and the warmth felt good on her skin. She strode into the building, immediately appreciating the security a manned front desk provided. He checked her ID and directed her to the fourth floor where *Mr. Sterling* would be waiting to show her around.

Mr. Sterling was in for a huge surprise.

JARED LOOKED AROUND the four-bedroom apartment, appreciating how the light streamed through the windows in the morning. Charlotte would wake up to sunshine while having her morning coffee. Assuming she enjoyed caffeine to start the day. He didn't know even the most minute detail about her, yet he wondered.

His phone rang at the same time a knock sounded on the door he'd unlocked for Charlotte.

"Come in!" he called out before answering the call, which, of course, was from work.

He couldn't take one damned morning off without them needing him for something but Brooke wouldn't bother him if it wasn't important. He listened to her explain the issue as Charlotte walked into the room, and he couldn't stop staring. She wore a pair of black, tight leggings that molded to her long legs and a fitted, pink V-neck short-sleeve shirt. Her hair brushed her shoulders and that familiar kick of desire rushed through him.

"Hi," she said, and he reluctantly gestured toward the phone he had pressed to his ear.

Charlotte nodded, acknowledging he was on the phone, and began her own walk through the empty space he'd hoped to bring alive in his description as he showed her around.

He listened to Brooke explain that a scandal had broken out with Randalls, one of the companies they'd recently invested in and recommended to their clients. The stock was tanking and the question of whether to bail or ride it out sat on Jared and Alex's shoulders and he needed to take a Zoom call.

"I'll join from my home office. Give me five minutes." He disconnected the call and walked over to where Charlotte stood looking out the kitchen window he'd been admiring earlier. "Beautiful view, isn't it?"

She nodded but he was really looking at her profile.

"Listen, I hate to do this but I have a work emergency. Would you mind waiting up in my apartment while I take a Zoom call there?" he asked.

"This is your building?" Surprise lit her gaze, her eyes opening wide. "I thought we'd start at some of the others Fallon mentioned."

He shook his head. "As it turns out, there were new leases I wasn't aware of and this building is the only one with free units."

"Oh. I see."

He stepped closer, aware he was needed by the office but unable to resist another minute with her. "Do you have concerns about living in the same building as me?"

She turned to face him. "Of course not. I can handle you." She treated him to a saucy smile. "But seriously about today, if you need to reschedule—"

His phone pinged, reminding him the office was waiting.

He shook his head. "No. I'll handle this and get right back to you. At least at my place you'll have somewhere comfortable to sit."

"Okay then. Lead the way."

Up at Jared's apartment, which just happened to be the penthouse, the elevator doors opened and they walked into his personal space.

"Make yourself at home," he said, rushing off and down a hallway to do business.

Make yourself at home, she mused, looking around the massive space. Even the apartment she'd briefly looked at downstairs was larger than she'd anticipated. She did not want to take advantage of Noah, no matter how big his trust fund. She'd asked for four bedrooms. What did she expect? She could downsize to two, forcing the girls to share even in the teen years, but she just knew once Noah found out she was pregnant, he would still insist the twins had room options.

With a sigh, she walked through the living area of the apartment that boasted neutral modern furniture and expansive views. But what drew her attention were the artifacts on floating wall shelves. Walking closer, she eyed the Incan pottery she had no doubt was original, made from natural clay mixed with sand, rock, and shell to prevent cracking.

He had what must be a museum-grade Roman dodecahedron replica, a small, hollow, twelve-sided object, the exact use of which was still unknown. And a stone casting of Ishtar, also known as Astarte, the Babylonian goddess of war and fertility, among other pieces.

"Fascinating," she murmured, impressed by both his collection and taste in art. Who knew they had so much in common? He'd never mentioned his interest in archaeology but clearly he had an appreciation for ancient artifacts.

She settled onto a comfortable couch and went through her phone, checking mail, social media, and texts. She hoped to hear from her brother, the only family she kept in touch with, but he'd been silent since she'd been home. Not that she was surprised. He had his share of troubles in his life and she hoped everything was okay.

When she ran out of things to do, she began to read a mystery novel she'd started. A blaring car horn startled her, and she jumped and glanced at the time on her phone. She'd been here for an hour. Though she understood Noah had an emergency, she didn't want to sit here waiting. Swiping through her phone screen, she found the Uber app, intending to send for a ride.

"Shit, I am so sorry." Jared joined her, looking more harried than when he'd left.

This time he had been running his fingers through his hair and hers itched to do the same. Clearly, it was time to get out of here. "I was just about to go home. You're busy and I don't want to take you away from something important." She already knew the pressure he was under to take the bulk of the firm's workload from his father.

"No. Please stay. Brooke has it all under control. Do you want to go see the apartment?" He glanced at his watch and grimaced. "How about we order something to eat, check out the apartment, and by the time it gets here, it'll be lunchtime."

She shook her head. "It's fine. I got a quick glimpse while you were on the phone and it's gorgeous, but it's honestly going to be out of my budget."

He glanced at her, amusement in his gaze, his sexy lips lifting in a smile. "How do you even know what the rent is? We haven't discussed it."

She didn't want to play games. "Fine. How much is it?"

He gave her a number that was absolutely too low and he was obviously doing her a favor. She wanted to snap at him that she didn't need charity but held the words back. He was attempting to be a nice guy and probably trying not to rip off his brother-in-law, assuming he knew Noah was helping her out for the girls' sake. Her independence and ability to take care of her twins meant everything to her. Accepting help from Noah was bad enough.

Instead of letting her embarrassment get the better of her, she drew in and released a deep breath before speaking. "I know you're trying to help but I couldn't take it for that price. We both know it's worth way more than that."

"It might be, but I'd rather have a tenant I know and like than someone who could be a pain in the ass right below me." He wiggled his eyebrows and she laughed, breaking the tension as she suspected was his intent.

"Just tell me you'll consider it. Give it some real thought."

Inside, her stomach twisted but she nodded. "I'll think about it."

He placed a hand on her shoulder, and she felt his heated touch through the fabric of her top. Their gazes locked and awareness settled between them. In fact, she actually felt like the air crackled with static electricity, the sparks between them were so potent.

He stepped closer and tilted his head down, his intent clear, and she panicked.

"Don't!" she exclaimed, unable to let him kiss her before he knew the truth.

Confusion wrinkled his brows. "What's wrong?"

"I'm pregnant," she blurted out, watching as his eyes opened wide and the implications of her statement dawned.

He stepped back, grasping onto the back of the nearest chair. "And it's—"

"Yours."

He sucked in a startled breath. A few seconds passed in silence as he processed what she'd said. He glanced at her still flat stomach in disbelief and tried to swallow though his throat had gone dry. "Holy shit."

At least he hadn't asked if she was certain he was the father. She didn't think she could have handled that humiliation.

"I need to sit down," he said, and she gestured to the sofa.

He lowered himself to the seat and she kept quiet, giving him the space she assumed he needed. With butterflies in her stomach, she waited for his reaction.

Chapter Six

JUST WHEN JARED thought his life couldn't get more complicated. *He was going to be a father.* He stared at nothing, trying to sort out his feelings. Was he startled? Yes. Worried about how his life was going to change? No doubt about it. Concerned about making time when work was so all-consuming? That, too.

But at his core he was a pragmatist. How else could he be living and breathing business, other than the basic reason? His family needed him to step up and he'd had no choice. But he was going to have to look deeper now because he wasn't letting Charlotte go through this alone. He might be stunned but he knew the kind of man he was. He'd step up.

But why *were* they going through this to begin with? She'd said she had an IUD and she didn't strike him as the type to lie. "So… I have to ask. How?"

She twisted her hands in front of her, not meeting his gaze. "Apparently my IUD failed because it was due to be changed. I thought I was covered. I honestly did. I mean, who does this… twice?" She gestured to her still flat stomach.

"Hey. Come sit." He patted the cushion beside him.

She lowered herself onto the sofa, holding herself stiff and apart.

"Relax. I'm not angry. Surprised and in shock? Yeah. But you can breathe." Reaching out, he rubbed her back in comforting circles and she expelled a long stream of air.

She finally met his gaze and in her eyes he saw warmth and gratitude. "How did I get this lucky... twice? Noah was a gentleman about it, and now you?" She shook her head in disbelief.

"What *did* happen with Noah?" He'd never thought to ask, and now that he had? He realized he was actually jealous of his brother-in-law because he'd been with Charlotte first.

"Well, we were both in Toronto, me at a conference, and we met in the airport while waiting for our flight home. A massive snowstorm came through and the airline put us up at a hotel. One thing led to another... We used a condom but... I won't say we were unlucky because I love my girls."

He really disliked hearing about her night with Noah, but he'd asked, so he set his jaw and continued to listen.

"It was just one of those things that happened. Once in a lifetime, at least that's what I assumed at the time." Her lips twisted in a wry smile. "But here we are."

"Here we are. I hope you don't mind me asking but were you and Noah ever… involved?"

Her light laughter filled the room. "No. We were tipsy, there was a brief attraction but we agreed from the beginning all either of us wanted to do was co-parent."

He couldn't deny being relieved. Then again, considering his sister and Noah's relationship, and how much Fallon liked Charlotte, he'd never considered her an issue for either of them. He put those thoughts out of his head and focused on the present.

"Have you known you were pregnant for a while?" Because he'd known for five minutes and he was reeling.

She shook her head. "Not really. I took a test before I left the dig site and I planned on telling you when we were alone. I just had to find the right way to do it."

He recalled being about to kiss her when she'd blurted out the news. "You definitely did that."

Her cheeks flushed pink. "Sorry. I wasn't really thinking, but I didn't want things to get more complicated between us before you knew about the baby." She rested her hands on her stomach and a weird sensation settled in his chest.

"Are we complicated?" he asked, rubbing where it felt like heartburn and not an overwhelming rush of emotion. It had to be too soon for that. Right?

"We shouldn't be. We should be smart about this. Figure out how we want to handle things."

He narrowed his gaze. "Handle things? As in whether or not to keep the baby?" he asked, unable to keep the accusation from his tone.

He'd only known about the pregnancy for a short time but he was already coming to accept his life was about to go in a whole new direction. And the moment he thought she might take that away, he realized he was okay with the big change that was coming his way. He didn't want her to make a choice that would rid him of the option of being a parent.

"No, I'm not debating whether or not to keep the baby, although that decision is mine to make. My body, my choice," she said firmly.

He nodded, relieved. "For the record, I agree. It just wasn't a direction I wanted you to take."

"I'm glad you feel that way. And I'm relieved you know. At least I can put that worry to rest."

"You can," he said, as he rose to his feet. "Now, can I order lunch and feed you? You're eating for two." He grinned and her easy smile lifted the weight that had settled in his stomach during their conversation.

She shook her head. "Thanks, but I'm tired. This whole reveal wore me out. I'm going to go back to my hotel and take a nap."

He really didn't want her staying at a hotel when he had an apartment right downstairs just waiting for her to say yes. She'd already figured out he'd knocked down the rent, but she didn't know he and Noah had talked and agreed on a number they thought she might eventually accept. He knew her independence was important to her and now wasn't the time to push. On anything.

She stood and walked toward him. He held out his arms and she stepped into his embrace. He pulled her against him, resting his chin on her head. She fit right, he thought, aware he was getting ahead of himself. She needed time to adjust to their new reality and the truth was, so did he.

"We're in this together," he reassured her, drawing a deep breath and inhaling her arousing, sweet yet sexy, floral scent.

Noah might have been fine being her co-parent, but Jared was going to have a much harder time keeping things *uncomplicated* between them.

JARED WALKED CHARLOTTE to the elevator in his apartment and accompanied her downstairs. He waited until she was safely in an Uber before heading upstairs and texting his brother, Aiden. If there was anyone who could help him process his current situation, it was the sibling he was closest to. Luckily, Aiden was still in town.

His brother suggested they meet up at Remy's bar, but Jared didn't want anyone else in the family intruding. He proposed Club Ten29, an upscale nightclub owned by Jason Dare, a cousin of Remy's partner at The Back Door, Zach Dare. They agreed on the place and time, four p.m.

Jared spent the rest of the afternoon at the office, finding it difficult to concentrate and glad Brooke had taken over this morning's issue with the stock. His father had dealt with the business news calmly, at least for Alex when he was worked up, and Jared managed to get him to take a step back. He'd be dealing with some low maintenance clients this afternoon. Meanwhile, Jared stared at his computer screen, unable to get any work done, and was grateful when it was time to leave to meet Aiden.

It took him thirty minutes to get downtown by the company car service. He walked inside and took in the décor. He liked the vibe of the club, the glass wall behind the bar lined with liquor bottles and the dim lighting.

His brother sat at a table, a glass of what was probably scotch in his hand.

Jared joined him, finding a glass of liquor waiting for him. "Thanks," he said, sitting down and taking a much-needed sip.

Aiden, wearing a pair of jeans and a Henley, looked relaxed, unlike how Jared was feeling. "What's got you so frazzled you wanted to meet in the middle of the workday? Is it the business? Dad?"

"Dad's fine," he reassured his brother. "Not so sure about me. I'm going to be a father."

Aiden burst out laughing. "Good one. Now what's the real reason we're here?"

Jared kept his serious face on, pulling his mouth tight before speaking. "I," he said, gesturing to himself, "am going to be a father."

"Shit. You're serious. I didn't think you had time for sex."

He shook his head because his brother had a point. "I don't. It was the night of Fallon's wedding. Not *at* the wedding. After the wedding. Except we might have gone upstairs early."

"You fucked a bridesmaid?" Aiden asked.

"That's so cliché. It was Charlotte. Charlie." Charlotte seemed to be his name for her and his alone.

"You fucked—"

"Hey, watch it. Don't talk about her like that."

Aiden's eyes opened wide. "So you still have feelings for her and you knocked her up." He held up his hands. "I mean, you got her pregnant."

"Better. And yeah." He raised his glass and Aiden did the same. They took a drink and set them on the table.

"Can I ask you something? Did you kids ever hear of condoms? Or, I don't know, abstinence?" He waved a hand. "Sorry, I shouldn't joke. But seriously. Charlie? She accidentally got pregnant… twice in one lifetime?"

Jared ran a hand across his face. "Apparently, she and Noah used a condom. No idea what happened there. And with me, she was at the end life of her IUD and didn't know."

Aiden slowly nodded. "Okay, all kidding aside. How are you doing?"

"I'd say I reacted well, so one point for me. I'm not as freaked out as I should be and I don't understand why."

His brother swirled his drink and studied him. "I think I do."

Jared cocked an eyebrow, waiting for the answer.

"Like I said earlier, you have feelings for her. I could tell when we spoke at Dad's. You were protective of her just now and you call her Charlotte. Nobody calls her Charlotte. So because you're invested, the idea of a baby isn't freaking you out."

Instead of making a wisecrack, he let his brother's

words settle. They were nothing he hadn't considered himself. In fact, he'd had the random thought that if he had to go through this with anyone, he was glad it was Charlotte.

He couldn't say this is the direction he saw his life going and it was going to take a lot of adjustment. But he was managing the news with some semblance of calm. The biggest thing on his mind at the moment was making the time he both needed and wanted for the changes coming in his life.

He looked at the brother who traveled the world but had recently hinted that he might want to give up the danger.

"Aiden… I'm going to need help at work."

"Good, because I want to come home."

Jared let out a relieved breath, the tightening in his chest loosening at his brother's intent. "Thank God. I'm tired of worrying about you. You'll come work at Sterling?"

"Yeah. You've been bearing the brunt of Dad's illness alone and for too long. I need time to wrap up some things abroad but I'll be back. This time for good."

With a nod, Jared said, "I have one more favor."

"Name it."

"Don't tell the family about Charlotte until I'm ready to do it myself." He didn't know if she was going to tell the twins and he wanted to talk to her before he blurted it out to everyone. Especially Fallon and Noah. She might want to handle that herself, since it involved telling her girls.

"You got it," Aiden promised. "Same for me coming home. I need to do it in my own time and my own way."

Jared grinned. "Whatever you need. I'm just glad to have you back." And not just because he wanted help at work. He'd really missed his brother.

AFTER LEAVING JARED'S, Charlie went to her hotel and took a nap, something she'd needed more frequently lately. She remembered the exhaustion from her pregnancy with the twins and when she could, she gave in to the need and slept.

As soon as she woke up, feeling more refreshed, the morning's events came back to her and her dilemma with the apartment swirled in her head.

Not wanting to think about it and torture herself with what to do, she called her BFF, Leo Watson. They'd met when sharing a table at a coffee shop, both working on their laptops. She'd been on a break from the museum, pre-dig, and Leo, a financial analyst, had also been taking a breather from the office. They'd gotten to talking and had been friends ever since.

Their relationship had always been purely platonic and he was like the brother she wished her sibling, Dan, could have been. Leo had been her first call once she'd returned to the States. After the twins, that was. Though she had girl friends from her old job at the museum where she'd worked before going to Egypt, she felt closest to Leo. She'd even told him she was pregnant when her own brother didn't know.

She'd tried calling Dan and left a message, but she still hadn't heard back. It was just like her sibling not to call. He was too self-absorbed and always making wrong choices to be there for her or to give her the chance to help him. He worked when he could as a salesman or delivery guy, but usually got fired because he didn't show up on time or at all.

Tonight, she needed a shoulder and a wise opinion, so she'd called Leo and said she needed a friends' night, sweetening the deal by promising to bring ice cream for her and a six-pack of beer for him. He could drink; she couldn't. So vanilla fudge it was.

She took a taxi to his building, walked up one flight, and knocked on his door. He greeted her, immediately pulling her into a hug.

"How'd it go with the baby daddy?" he asked, concern in his tone.

"Jared was so nice," she said and burst into tears.

Leo wrapped an arm around her, patting her back, then bringing her into him. She absorbed the much-needed hug before stepping away. "I'm okay. Just overly emotional."

He nodded in understanding, taking the bag with the six-pack and the ice cream. "Come in and we'll talk."

She followed him into the apartment and to the kitchen, where he grabbed a bowl and spoon. He scooped out the ice cream, handed it to her, took a beer, and they settled in the family room on the sofa across from the massive TV.

"Tell me about what happened this morning," Leo said.

Skipping the part about how she'd blurted out the pregnancy news before Jared could kiss her, she explained what a gentleman Jared had been and how she'd lucked out twice.

"Then why the tears?" Leo asked.

She dug out a spoonful of ice cream and savored the flavor before answering. "I'm overwhelmed. The apartment issue is hanging over my head. Either I'm on a corner bordering a not-so-great area or I'm in a luxury building in an apartment Jared knocked the rent way down on, doing me a favor." She continued to eat as they spoke. "Don't get me wrong, I'm so grateful and I'm aware of how fortunate I am. But I hate feeling like a burden."

Leo shrugged. "Is a favor really so bad? It doesn't seem like it's an issue for him or he wouldn't lower the price. And same with Noah, who you said offered to help out."

"I have pride, you know. I want to feel like I can support the girls on my own." Without relying on a man who might one day decide to opt out of her life.

She placed the empty bowl on the table, spoon inside.

Leo shifted so he was facing her. "Not every man is your father, Charlie. Noah's been rock solid for more than ten years. What makes you think Jared won't be?" he asked, ever the voice of reason.

But he didn't know what being abandoned felt like. "I just want to feel like if something changes, I won't be in a bind with nowhere to go."

Leo rolled his eyes.

"Don't do that. I'm serious."

"So am I. You didn't make any of these children alone. Their fathers are willing to step up. Swallow your pride and let them."

She swallowed hard. "I'll give it serious thought." Though it hurt her need for independence, she had a hunch that ultimately she'd have to give in so her girls were in a good place.

Which would put her in close proximity with Jared, the man she couldn't get out of her mind for reasons that had nothing to do with her having his baby.

Chapter Seven

DESPITE THE MORNING sickness Charlie couldn't shake, which surfaced on and off all day, she took the girls to the Museum of Natural History, as promised. Dylan loved the Butterfly Vivarium where she saw hundreds of species. Dakota, naturally, flipped over the pupae incubator where she viewed chrysalises and watched butterflies emerge. Thanks to Egypt, Charlie was used to the eighty percent humidity in the enclosure, but it didn't help her queasy stomach or dizziness.

She sat with the girls while they shared a cheese panini and she sipped on a cup of iced decaffeinated tea. After the space show and movie, which were hits, they toured the dinosaur exhibit, a place Charlie used to frequent with her own mother.

She also used to bring the girls before she left for Egypt. It warmed her heart to be able to share the foundation of her love for archaeology with her children, and it gave them something unique to bond over.

Once their long day ended, she brought the girls back to Noah's for the night. Charlie had a meeting scheduled with Jared to do a final walk through the available apartment and make a decision, but she wanted to talk to Noah first.

Once at Noah and Fallon's, Charlie turned to Fallon. "Can you take the girls to get something to eat? I need to discuss a few things with Noah." She didn't mean to exclude Fallon but she needed the privacy from the kids.

"Little ears," Dakota said with an eye roll.

"Yep. The parents need to talk," Dylan chimed in.

A grin lifted Fallon's lips at their word play and she glanced at the twins. "Who wants homemade cookies?"

"Me!"

"I do!"

Putting a hand on their backs, Fallon quickly herded the girls into the kitchen, leaving Charlie and Noah alone.

"Are you okay?" he asked.

She nodded. "But I need to tell you something and because you know me better than most, I also need your opinion."

"Okay. Do you want to sit?" He gestured to the family room.

"I'd rather pace," she said, and began to walk back and forth in the entryway, keeping an eye on him when she strode his way.

He leaned against the wall, studying her. "Okay, I'm braced. Let's hear it."

"I'm pregnant and I'm telling you because you're the twins' father and when I'm ready to explain it to them, you'll need to know."

His eyes grew wide. "Holy shit, Charlie."

She wrapped her arms around herself and nodded. "My thoughts exactly."

"Are you… happy about it?" he asked, sounding genuinely concerned.

She nodded. "I've had some time to let it settle and, yes, I'm happy. Thrown and shaken, but excited."

He treated her to a smile. "Then I'm happy for you. And I can help talk to the girls when the time comes. Or you can handle it yourself. Your decision." He paused, then said, "You also said you needed my advice?"

She bit down on the inside of her cheek. "When I leave here, I'm meeting Jared to look at the apartment in his building. He gave me a rental amount that was definitely not the going rate. It gives me a financial break, it gives you a break… and he takes the hit. You know how I feel about standing on my own two feet."

Noah tapped his foot against the floor, obviously in thinking mode. "You should know I spoke to him this morning. I knew about the rent."

She narrowed her gaze. "Is that all he told you?"

she asked warily, wondering if Jared had shared the pregnancy news and Noah was pretending to be surprised.

"What else is there?" Noah asked, genuinely confused.

Without thinking, her hand went to her stomach, partly because she was nauseous and in part in reflex.

As soon as he caught the gesture, Noah's lips parted, his shock obvious. "Jared's the father?" he asked in a hushed whisper.

She nodded.

"Jesus." He ran a hand through his hair as the surprises kept coming.

"What?" she asked. "It's not like we're blood-related. God, would you relax?"

"Hey, you startled me. At least now I know why he's being so generous with the rent," he said.

She shook her head. "Technically, he was being generous even before he knew about the baby."

Noah nodded. "Okay, then. That brings me to that advice you want. I know you and I'm sure I know what you're asking, so here's my answer. Take the apartment."

"But—"

He stepped closer and placed a friendly hand on her shoulder. "Put aside your pride and concerns. It's good for you, good for the girls. The area is beyond safe, there's a doorman, and I'll feel better knowing that's where you're all sleeping at night."

As close as she and Noah were, he didn't know the cause of her insecurities, her past with her parents… they weren't emotionally connected in any way but through the twins. As for the apartment… "Leo said to take it, too."

"He's right." After all these years, Noah knew her best friend, having met him many times.

She nodded. "And I know that I should be more grateful to you and to Jared. So thank you again for the financial help, Noah. And the advice."

"Of course. If you need anything, Fallon and I are here for you." He paused. "I have to tell her, you know that, right?"

"Yeah. I understand. I'll let Jared know his sister knows. Life really can change in an instant," she said with a shake of her head.

Noah chuckled. "That it can. In your case, twice."

She rolled her eyes, mimicking Dakota's favorite gesture. "Let's not go there, okay?" Charlie turned toward the kitchen. "Girls, come say bye!"

After getting her hugs, Charlie said so long to Noah and Fallon, and went downstairs to meet the Uber she'd sent for. Next stop, Jared Sterling's place.

She sat in the back of the car in stop-and-go traffic, the movement of the vehicle combined with her morning sickness working to increase the nausea and dizziness she'd already been feeling. She texted Jared as they turned the corner on which his building was located, as he'd wanted to meet her downstairs and take her up to the apartment.

By the time the driver pulled up to the curb, she was so relieved to be getting out of the vehicle for fresh air, she thought she might cry.

Pulling herself together, she thanked the driver and exited the car. She stepped out of the vehicle as Jared walked through the doors and strode toward her.

She paused and breathed in fresh, though warm and humid, air, fighting the dizziness. Just a few more seconds and she'd be in an air-conditioned space and feel better, she assured herself.

When she recovered enough, she started toward Jared just as another wave of nausea and dizziness assaulted her, black spots circling in front of her eyes. She reached for him but stumbled and fell against his chest, Jared's strong arms wrapping around her. Without warning, her knees buckled, before everything went black.

JARED WATCHED CHARLOTTE exit the vehicle and he strode to meet her. She paused and wobbled despite not wearing heels, so he picked up his stride to get to her faster. She suddenly reached for him, staggering and falling into him. His heart skipped a beat, grateful he was close enough to catch her.

He wrapped his arms around her and just as he thought she was safe, her knees buckled and she started to go down. He scooped her into his arms and rushed toward the building.

The doorman held open the entry and Jared strode inside, sitting down with her in his arms.

"Charlotte?" He patted her cheeks, his heart beating too fast in his chest. "Charlie." He resorted to her nickname. Anything to wake her up. He glanced at the doorman. "Ronald, call an ambulance. Tell them she's pregnant."

"Yes, Mr. Sterling."

"Charlotte," he said again.

"No ambulance," she said as she blinked her eyes and began to regain consciousness.

Relief filled him and he took his first full breath since watching her stumble. "Sorry, sweetheart. You fainted and you're pregnant. That means you're going to get checked out by a doctor." He needed to know the baby was fine and so was she.

"They're on their way," Ronald said from his position behind the desk.

Given they were in New York City, the sirens

sounded fairly quickly and two paramedics rushed into the lobby. They took her pulse, blood pressure, and oxygen levels before they walked out and returned with a stretcher.

"Is this really necessary?" she asked, as she was settled on the gurney.

"We want to make sure the baby is okay," Jared said.

She placed her hand on her flat stomach. "Okay. I agree. We need to check on the baby." She turned her head away from him.

He glanced up at the paramedics. "I'm coming with her," he said without asking for permission, but demanding it.

"Ma'am?" They looked to Charlotte.

She nodded. "He's concerned about his baby. Let him come."

He narrowed his eyes. He was worried about her too. Before he could give her comment much thought, he was following the stretcher and getting into the ambulance for the ride to the hospital.

They were brought through to the ER and settled Charlotte in a room. Someone came to do intake forms, a nurse checked her vitals, and after forty minutes of uncomfortable silence because Charlotte didn't have much to say, a doctor arrived, pushing a machine with her.

"Hello. I'm Dr. Messing, an OB-GYN. I understand you fainted. I'd like to ask you some questions, okay?"

Charlotte nodded. "Of course."

The doctor, an attractive woman with red hair pulled back in a bun, stepped closer to the edge of what the ER considered a bed.

"How far along are you?"

Charlotte wrinkled her nose as she thought. "About two months."

"And how has your pregnancy been? Nausea? Dizziness?" she asked Charlotte.

Charlotte let out a small laugh. "Lots of nausea and not just in the morning. The dizziness didn't happen until today."

The doctor smiled in understanding. "That nausea is very normal."

Charlotte grinned. "Oh, I had twins. I'm well aware of pregnancy symptoms."

The doctor's eyes opened wide. "A pro then. Good. Was that an otherwise typical pregnancy?"

She nodded.

"And did you eat today?"

She sighed and Jared knew the answer. He let out low noise, frustrated she wasn't taking care of herself.

"I understand you don't feel great but you need to keep up your strength and not let your blood sugar levels drop. Have you seen an obstetrician yet?"

She nodded. "I just got back to this country two weeks ago and it was a priority."

"Okay, I want to do an ultrasound and check the baby. Is this the father?" she asked, glancing at Jared.

"Yes. He can stay," Charlotte murmured.

"Wonderful." The doctor began to set up the machine, plugging it in and preparing the wand. "Okay, Mom and Dad, let's find the baby's heartbeat."

Charlotte pulled up the thin gown she'd changed into when they arrived and drew a deep breath.

His gaze on her pale stomach, Jared stepped closer and instinctively grasped her hand. She curled her fingers around his and he took note of the roughness on the pads, no doubt caused by her work. He couldn't help but admire the dedication it must take to sift through sand to find ancient artifacts.

"Here we go." The doctor's voice drew his focus back to the ultrasound.

Whooshing noises sounded around them as she moved the wand over Charlotte's belly. She squeezed his hand tighter and he put his free hand on her shoulder.

Suddenly, a fast, thumping sound surrounded them and the doctor smiled. "Aah, here we go. A nice, fast, healthy heartbeat."

A lump formed in his throat, the pregnancy becoming real for the first time. That was his baby's heartbeat. His and Charlotte's. Excitement and happiness filled him in ways he'd never experienced before.

"Look," Dr. Messing said, turning a black-and-white screen toward them. She pointed out various things he wouldn't have recognized, a gestational sac, the yolk sac, umbilical cord, and, finally, the fetus.

His future.

He looked at Charlotte, who had happy tears in her eyes, as she met his gaze.

His *whole* future.

Chapter Eight

O VER AN HOUR later, Charlotte found herself in Jared's apartment, her feet up on the sofa, blanket over her legs. He'd prepared dinner and was catering to her every need and she wasn't sure how to feel about all the attention.

She was well aware his priority was making sure the baby was okay, which the doctor had reassured them, it was. Though she knew fainting could be normal in pregnancy, she was still reassured.

She'd passed out due to low sugar, made worse by her skipping lunch. She was pretty sure Jared had let out a low, sexy growl when he'd heard that news. For some reason, his reaction had gone a long way to soothe her insulted ego when he'd seemed to be more worried about the baby than her.

She knew in her heart she was overreacting but that moment was a reminder of her core issue. She might be developing feelings for Jared, but she'd never know if he desired her for herself or because she was carrying his baby.

He strode into the room with a tray filled with food and set it down across from her. He'd rolled up his sleeves, revealing muscular forearms. His hair was that messy style she loved.

"Your dinner is served. And so is mine." He settled in beside her, so close she smelled his familiar, sexy cologne, which always managed to arouse her.

She glanced at the food. "Thank you, but I told you I had crackers at the hospital."

"Crackers isn't a meal. You heard the doctor say you need to eat to keep up your strength. Though I shouldn't admit this, Lizzie sends me home with dinners, so I've got apricot chicken and mashed potatoes for you."

Her stomach rumbled and she blushed. "I guess I am hungry." And she felt like she could hold down this meal, which looked delicious. "Thank you," she murmured.

They didn't speak as they ate and to her surprise, she gobbled down her food, finishing all but one spoonful she couldn't possibly find room for.

"One more bite?" He picked up her fork and placed the food on the tines, holding it out for her.

She let out a groan. "Please tell me you're not going to be one of those hovering baby daddies?"

He shrugged. "What if I am? And it's not just about the baby. It's about me making sure you're taking care of yourself."

"Why?" Why did he care? And why did she have

this deep-seated need to know?

He placed all the dishes on the tray and moved it out of the way, then turned toward her, his knees touching hers. "Why? Because I haven't stopped thinking about you since the wedding? Because I think you're a special human being and I care about you?"

"Are those questions?" she asked, knowing she was being a wise-ass. But her defense mechanism kicked in, even as her heart filled with his words, making her feel better about her fears.

Not that they'd ever go away, but at least he said all the right things.

"Cute. But I'm serious and I want you to know that. You scared me today," he said, his tone more intense than she'd ever heard from him.

"I'm sorry. I didn't mean to skip a meal, it's just so hard when I'm not feeling well."

He nodded. "You need a keeper, Charlotte Kendall." He moved in closer and when she didn't object, leaned closer still until his lips hovered over hers.

She had no intention of stopping him. Not when he was everything she desired. Even if she planned to protect her heart, she couldn't deny wanting him.

He kissed her and she leaned into him, kissing him back. With a groan, he slid his hand through the back of her hair and tipped her head, holding her in place while he plundered her mouth.

One thing about Jared. The man knew how to kiss. His tongue swirled around hers and it wasn't long before she was lost. He pulled her bottom lip into his mouth, releasing it with a pop and soothing the skin with sensual licks.

He lifted his head and she moaned at the loss but he clearly had a plan as he turned her body, easing her down on the sofa. She went willingly and he maneuvered her so her head was at the top of the couch and her legs draped over his.

He slid his hand inside the leggings she'd been forced to wear because her jeans no longer fit, and rubbed his fingers over her sex.

"Jared," she moaned, enjoying the sensation of his strong fingers strumming her pussy over her panties. It wasn't enough. She needed to feel him directly on her skin and she arched her lower back, seeking further contact.

With his other hand, he slapped her there and she jumped in surprise, the even bigger shock following when warmth traveled through her lower body.

"I'll give you what you need," he said in a firm voice that also turned her on.

"Can you hurry then? I need to come," she said, hearing the plea in her voice and not caring a bit.

"Lift," he said, and she raised her hips, allowing him to work her leggings and panties down. He slid his fingers back to her sex. Using his forefinger, he rubbed her entrance. "You're wet for me." His voice was gruff and she liked it. His slick finger began to rub over her clit, as he worked her body like an instrument only he knew how to play.

Back and forth, then slow circles, his touch aroused while inside she felt empty and needy. Unable to stay still, she circled her hips in time to his motions and the sensations began to rise inside her body.

"I…"

"What? Tell me," he said, pinching the tight bud and releasing it quickly.

She moaned again. "I need you inside me."

"I need to be delicate with you after what you've been through today, but I can help." He slipped one finger inside her, pumping in and out until she was wetter and slicker, before adding a second finger.

She arched her head back and her lower body lifted, pulling him farther inside her.

He curled his fingers and began to rub at a sensitive spot she'd heard of but never believed existed. "Oh my God." Spots appeared behind her eyes, and not the dizzy kind.

"That's it, sweetheart. Soon." He pumped his fingers, hitting the right place each time he went deep, and soon she was screaming out an orgasm. One that had her seeing stars and losing herself to his perfect ministrations.

She came back to herself slowly. She didn't re-member him pulling out his fingers but when she opened her eyes, he was sucking in the two digits, and wow, that was hot.

"Feel better?" he asked.

"Much," she said, more languid and relaxed than she'd been in far too long.

He chuckled, a satisfied smile on his face despite the hard ridge of his cock pressing against her bottom.

"You scared me today," he repeated. He swiped her hair off her cheek and stroked her skin with his other hand. "Promise me you'll eat three meals a day and snacks?"

"I promise to do the best I can." Her voice felt thick, her entire body still a gelatinous mess.

He nodded. "Fair enough. Move in with me," he said.

Despite the relaxed state she'd been in, she pushed herself back and sat upright on the sofa. "Have you lost your mind?" she asked him, ignoring the hand-some smirk on his face. "Tell me you didn't try and use my orgasm as a means to get what you wanted."

He lifted his shoulders and shrugged. "It seemed like as good a time as any to ask. I've got four bed-rooms. The office is in the second, you can take the third and the girls can share the fourth when they're with you. And by the time you have the baby, I'll have found us a bigger place to live."

She blinked, feeling like she'd entered an alternate universe. "Jared, we barely know each other."

"And what better way to do that than live together? After what happened today, I don't want you to be alone. I'd feel much better if I were around."

She drew in a deep breath and let it out again. "Today was a freak thing. I'll watch what I eat. I pushed myself because I'd promised the girls I'd take them to the museum, but I won't do that again."

"But—"

"No buts! I've lived alone my entire adult life. I got through a pregnancy with twins and have been raising the girls just fine without a second parent on the premises." She heard herself getting worked up but she was feeling pressured and never responded well to pressure. "Listen, I appreciate the offer, but there's no need."

Charlie was independent by necessity. As nice as it sounded to let Jared take care of her, it wasn't in her personality to trust that easily.

He groaned, but she heard him accepting defeat in the sound. "Then I want you to take the downstairs apartment so you're close by. Fair enough?"

Since she'd already come to terms with doing just that, she nodded. "Yes. I appreciate what you're doing for me and the baby." Their little life being the sole reason he was in this with her at all.

"Thank you, Charlotte."

"You're welcome." She glanced down and realized she was still undressed. Her cheeks flaming, she slid her feet off his lap and rose, pulling up her pants without meeting his gaze.

"I really need to go home. It's been a long day."

He stood, looking not the least bit flustered while she knew she must be a mess. "Let me know when you want to move in. I'll take the day off and arrange things with the building manager. He'll set aside an elevator for a couple of hours."

She rubbed her hands together, thinking about the logistics. "I have furniture in storage that I have to arrange to have moved. I'll need to call movers and it'll take me a bit to get things organized." She lifted her purse from the table and pulled out her phone.

"What are you doing?" he asked, stepping close.

She met his gaze. "Calling a rideshare."

"I'll take you home."

She shook her head. "There's no reason for you to go out again when I can get home easily."

"Not home, to the hotel, and I want to make sure you arrive at your room safely."

Her lips parted in surprise. "You're going to be overbearing for the next seven months, aren't you?"

He grinned. "I am. It's one of my finest qualities."

With a put-out sigh, she placed her phone back in her purse and gestured with one arm. "Lead the way."

He hooked his arm in hers. "My pleasure, sweetheart."

God, the man was potent with his hands and with his words. Pushing aside all her conflicting feelings, she let him put one hand on her back and steer her toward the garage.

JARED RETURNED FROM taking Charlotte back to the hotel and walking her to her room. After having his fingers in her pussy and her taste on his lips, going home alone had been cold comfort, but he was a man of patience. He'd take his time and do the old-fashioned thing. He'd woo her. Never in his life had he thought about slowly romancing a woman but Charlotte was different.

When she'd passed out in his arms, he'd been petrified, both for her and the baby. The idea of her moving in had been a spur-of-the-moment thought but it felt right at the time. It still did. But he understood why she'd rebelled against it. She was an independent spirit and he needed to respect that. If she ever moved in, it needed to be because they'd reached that point logically in their relationship. A relationship he wasn't sure she believed they had. Which was why he intended to show her how things could be.

In the meantime, he needed to tell his family about the baby. Charlotte had given her okay, and he had a choice. He could make the rounds to inform his siblings about his upcoming big life change one at a time or call for a family get-together. He opted for the latter and since he didn't want to reveal the news in a public place, he asked Lizzie and his dad if he could have everyone at the house on Saturday.

With everyone over, his father sat in his favorite recliner, the rest of his siblings and their significant others, minus Aiden, sat on the circular sofa in the family room, with a few in club chairs. Aiden had gone back abroad, planning to come home next month, and Jared had invited Brooke because she was family.

"Jared, are you going to explain why we're all here?" Remy asked, meeting his stare. "You said it was mandatory."

Raven sat beside him on the couch, her hand in his. "I'm curious, too."

"Who'd you knock up?" Dex asked with a chuckle, and his wife smacked his shoulder.

"Behave!" Samantha said.

Noah shook his head, remaining silent because he

and Fallon had already heard the news.

Jared rose to his feet. "Dex guessed it. I'm going to be a father."

"Damn! I should have taken bets," his brother said. "Are you serious?"

"Completely."

Chatter surrounded him as did shouted questions. Jared tuned them all out, waiting for silence.

He stared at his father, wondering what the older man was thinking. "Dad?"

"You're stepping up? Doing the right thing?" Alex asked.

Jared nodded. "Of course I am. The other news is about the baby's mother. It's Charlotte Kendall." He met Noah's gaze but found no judgment there. He supposed his brother-in-law had been in this exact same position almost a decade ago.

"Charlotte as in Charlie?" Remy asked. "You and Noah both…" He shook his head. "Never mind."

Noah had already winced.

"Yeah. Can we not go there? The fact is, she's pregnant with my baby and is going to move into the empty apartment in my building. At least she'll be close by. I just wanted to tell everyone at once. Not make the rounds."

"Well, I say congratulations!" Fallon rose, walked over, and pulled him into a hug. "We're going to have many small family gatherings." She laughed as she stepped back. "Seriously, though, you're going to make a great dad."

"Thanks, sis. I appreciate that."

"How are you going to handle the baby and work? You're at it twenty-four seven." Dex had risen to shake his hand, but he also asked a valid question.

He blew out a breath. "I'll figure it out," he said, knowing he'd promised Aiden not to reveal his plans to return home.

"I'm here for whatever you need at the office," Brooke said. "And I'm happy for you."

"Thanks. I'm going to take you up on that offer."

She smiled. "I expect you to."

The rest of the afternoon was spent talking to his siblings, answering questions, and being grateful for the type of family he was born into. Despite losing his mom, something he'd never get over, he had a solid parent in his dad, Lizzie who had stepped up as a maternal figure, never trying to replace their mother, and siblings just as happy to rib him as support him.

All things he could give to his baby. Knowing his child would be part of a close-knit family eased his mind about his fear of the unknown. None of these people would leave him floundering. His biggest challenge would be to bring Charlotte into the fold and convince her she belonged.

Chapter Nine

C HARLOTTE STEPPED OFF the hotel elevator and walked across the lobby to the concierge to see if she had any mail waiting for her. Though it had only been two weeks since she'd sent out résumés, she was anxious and hoping someone was impressed enough by her qualifications to offer her a position. She was hoping for an email, a phone call or a letter, though the last two were rare these days.

She stopped at the front desk where a familiar clerk smiled in recognition. "Hi, Ms. Kendall! What can I do for you today?"

"Hi, Patrick. I'm checking for packages or mail."

"I'll check for you." He walked into the back and returned with a few envelopes. "Here you go. Is there anything else I can do for you?"

She shook her head. "No, thanks. I appreciate it," she said, and immediately began sorting through the mail as she walked away. Nothing but junk, she thought, tossing the papers into the trash as she passed a garbage pail.

She stopped at the coffee shop for a cup of decaffeinated tea and headed up to her hotel room. She opened her laptop and loaded her emails. One in particular caught her eye. A curator position at a medium-sized museum not far from the building where she'd be living was interested in speaking to her. Right up her alley.

She wrote back immediately, agreeing to an interview. Now all she had to do was wait to hear back on a date and time. If she got this job then she'd feel much better about moving into the apartment in Jared's building. Like she was doing her part to pay some of the rent.

Excited, she forwarded the positive email to Leo along with a bunch of smiling emojis, not wanting to bother him at work by calling. Still on an emotional high, she tried her brother, surprised when he picked up the phone.

"Hello?" He sounded out of breath.

She was thrilled she'd reached him. "Hi, stranger! I've missed you. Did you get my message when I got back to the States?"

He paused, then said, "Sorry. I've been busy with some things."

"Too busy to reach out to your sister who you haven't seen in way too long?"

He let out an annoyed huff. "Did you call to give me shit?"

She rubbed the place above her heart, hurt by his

attitude. "No, I called to hear you voice."

"I'm sorry, sis. It's just not a good time."

She stiffened, certain he was looking for the easy way to earn drug money again. "Is everything okay?"

"I'm fine, but I have to go," he said and disconnected the call.

She stared at the phone in her hand, an uncomfortable feeling in the pit of her stomach. Her brother had a drug problem, one she didn't like to dwell on but knew enough to keep him away from her girls. They'd met their uncle Dan a few times when she knew he was clean, and she spoke of him, just telling the twins he worked hard and couldn't come see them. The only way she could manage day-to-day was by telling herself he was fine. Deep down, she knew better.

With nothing else to do and the girls busy with friends, she lay down to take a nap without setting an alarm. She and Noah were switching weeks and he had them this week. She stretched out on the bed and let her eyes drift closed…

THE RING OF her phone startled her awake. She fumbled for the cell, finding it on the night table. She glanced at the screen. *JARED STERLING.* She'd been tempted to change it out for *BABY DADDY*.

Wondering what he wanted, her stomach did a flip before she answered. "Hello?"

"Hi, Charlotte." The smooth way he said her full name set butterflies in her stomach.

"Jared."

She smiled at the formalities, amused when his deep chuckle reverberated through the phone, no doubt for the same reason. "What can I do for you?" she asked.

"Well, first off, how are you feeling?"

"I'm feeling better today. And you'll be happy to know I'm taking it easy. I was napping when you called."

"Shit. Sorry to wake you."

She'd glanced at the time when she answered the phone. "That's okay. I was out for two hours. I'll be lucky if I sleep tonight."

"Then maybe this is the perfect time to ask. Are you free for dinner?"

She pushed herself upright against the pillows and headrest. "Actually, I am. What did you have in mind?"

"I'd like to take you to Le Ciel Etoile in the Flatiron District."

French, translated to The Starry Sky in English. "That sounds amazing. I read about the restaurant in a travel magazine on my way home from Egypt." The place had a nod to the owner's native country, but was a steak restaurant with a French take on the classics.

"I'll pick you up at eight?"

"Sounds good," she said.

"Great. I'll see you soon."

"Yes," she murmured. "Bye." She disconnected the call and stared at the phone in her hand, the reality of her situation just now hitting her. A dressy dinner and she only had the late afternoon to figure out what to wear and to get ready.

She mentally crossed her fingers and called the salon downstairs, thrilled when they had an appointment for highlights, a trim, and a blow-dry. She hadn't had her hair touched since returning from her dig. They squeezed her in for a manicure as well.

She had twenty minutes before she had to be downstairs and she put her thoughts to her clothing. She wasn't certain what to wear, unsure if this were a date. Or was he taking her somewhere nice to discuss the baby? Her stomach gave a flutter at the possibility of a date but he hadn't specifically said. Still, it didn't hurt to look good either way.

She had a little black dress, but would it fit? Her waistline had popped and she doubted the garment would give her a sexy appearance, like she wanted.

Sexy?

Yes, she thought, sexy. If she was going out with Jared, she wanted him to look at her and like what he saw. There was a boutique in the hotel. She didn't know if her good luck would continue but she intended to find out.

An hour later, a short red dress was being sent to her room along with a pair of strappy sandals. Her nails were now a matching color, and she sat with foils in her hair. The stylist insisted caramel-colored highlights would go well with her skin tone. When the timer beeped, her hair was washed, trimmed, and styled. Her luck continued to hold and the in-house makeup artist had a cancelation.

She walked out of the salon feeling like a different woman. One that would, hopefully, take Jared's breath away.

JARED HAD TO call in favors to rent out the private room in the restaurant. Normally the smallest room seated ten, but he'd requested the space be emptied out and they put in a table for two.

The limousine he'd hired for the night stopped in front of the hotel. Though he'd planned on meeting Charlotte at her room, he walked into the lobby to find her waiting downstairs. She was looking at something in a store window, giving him a chance to take her in.

Red strappy sandals adorned her feet and she wore a short red dress with glittering material that wasn't fitted tight but draped her thighs and had him drooling. He couldn't see the swell of her stomach yet but she looked different to him.

She glowed and from the sonogram they'd seen, she was carrying his baby. The size of a bean, the heartbeat made it all so real, affecting him on a primal level. He felt possessive, both of the little bean and its mother.

As if she knew he was watching, Charlotte turned to face him, causing him to stop in his tracks and stare. Her hair fell to her shoulders in soft waves and caramel-colored highlights shimmered under the ceiling lights. The low-cut dress gave him the perfect view of ample cleavage but the coverage was still enough to tease not over-reveal.

It didn't matter that he'd seen her naked before. She left enough to his imagination to be sexy and his cock thickened in his pants. She'd always been gorgeous but knowing she was carrying his child made her irresistible.

She watched him approach, a smile on her red lips.

"Hello, beautiful."

A light flush stained her cheeks. "Hi, yourself, handsome."

He'd take the compliment.

"I appreciate you coming to get me but I could have met you at the restaurant," she said.

He held out an arm and she hooked hers with his.

"Then it wouldn't be a proper date, now would it?" He guided her to the exit and out of the building. He led her to the limousine where the driver held open the back door.

She stopped and stared. "Jared, where's your car? Or a rideshare?"

"Again, proper date." He stepped aside, gesturing for her to enter the vehicle, and he slid in beside her. A partition gave them plenty of privacy.

The driver shut the door and walked around, settling in his seat and starting the car.

Jared turned to Charlotte, who looked uncomfortable. He lifted a finger and twirled it in one of her curls. "Hey. Are you okay?"

She turned to face him and he dropped his hand. "I'm overwhelmed. By the lengths you went to today, the limo... I'm not used to this." She ran her hand up and down, indicating her entire outfit.

"I, for one, am glad you went to the extra effort, but you should know I think you're gorgeous with or without the glam."

She ducked her head. "Thank you."

"And the limo is because I want to wine and dine you, and make you feel special."

"Well, you are and I appreciate it. I'll stop making a big deal about it all." She leaned back in her seat and he draped an arm around her shoulders.

"It's going to take time to get downtown, so let's talk. Tell me more about you. Where did you grow up?"

"In a small town in Connecticut. Easy enough for Mom to take the train into the city when she worked. I told you about her."

He nodded. "And you mentioned you had a brother?"

"Dan. He tends to get into trouble and right now he's playing coy, so I haven't really spoken to him enough since I've been back." She twisted her fingers in her lap and he covered them with his hand.

"So he doesn't know you're pregnant?"

She shook her head.

"What about your father?" he asked.

She moved her head from side to side.

As she discounted family members, he realized how alone she was, especially compared to his large group of relatives. Even Lizzie and Brooke were family. But he wasn't only asking about hers because he wondered what her childhood was like. He was also curious about what had caused the walls she'd built and why they were so high.

She glanced out the window as the car made its

way downtown. "I don't like to talk about him," she murmured. "But so you know, because we're sharing a baby, my father won't be in our child's life."

"Okay. Do you speak to him at all?"

"No," she said, turning back to face him. "He wasn't there when I needed him after Mom died. I was sixteen and had lost my mother. I needed an adult, someone to turn to, to share my pain."

His chest hurt as she revealed her past trauma and he regretted asking. On the other hand, he was glad she'd shared this with him, that she'd let him in.

"I'm sorry. I know how hard it was for Fallon losing our mom when she was ten."

Her eyes grew soft. "I'm sorry I've been so selfish about my own past when yours—"

"Don't say, 'was so much worse'. There is no comparison when it comes to pain. You feel what you feel." He assumed she knew details about his mother from Fallon or Noah, but he intended to share his version of his childhood with her one day.

She nodded. "Can you tell me what happened?" Her big brown eyes pulled him in but it wasn't his time to unburden himself. It was still hers.

"I will. But not tonight. Let's finish the conversation about you. Your dad wasn't there for you how?"

"Let's just say his best friend was alcohol and still is."

Jared slid his hand into hers. "I'm sorry he didn't step up and do his job as your parent. You deserved better."

She treated him to a half smile. One that was sad. "You're damn right I did. And this little one is going to have everything they need." She cupped her stomach protectively and he placed his hand over hers.

"From both of us," he assured her, and hoped she believed him.

The vehicle came to a stop and Jared knocked on the divider, signaling he needed a minute.

"I know you'll be a good father," she said. "But there's something else I need you to know."

He raised an eyebrow. "What's that?"

"Though the baby and I are a package deal, you don't owe me anything. You especially don't owe me all this." She waved around the limousine.

He fought back the anger that rose inside him at the mere thought that she'd even believe he was dating her for the baby's sake. But he reminded himself she'd just told him she'd never been put first after her mother passed away. The man in her life who should have taken care of her had ignored her when she needed him most. Was it any wonder she didn't trust most guys to live up to their word?

"Charlotte, I'm not playing games with you. I'm not trying to get close to you for the sake of the baby.

I already trust you to allow me the privilege of being our child's father in every sense of the word."

She looked up at him with those big eyes. "Then why?"

"Because you interest me. I'm attracted to everything about you. Your face, your body, and your mind. And I want you to give me a chance to prove it."

Chapter Ten

ONCE INSIDE, THE maître d' led them past the crowded restaurant to the back. The chairs and tables were made of mahogany wood, which also lined the walls, and deep leather cushioned the seats. The lighting cast an amber glow, giving the room a yellow tint.

They stopped at a closed door, which when opened, led to a private room.

Jared surprised her at every turn.

She waited until they were seated and alone in the room before speaking. "Thank you but this is over-the-top! We could have had a table for two outside with everyone else."

He tapped her nose with his finger. "But then I wouldn't have you all to myself."

His comment affected her, warming her inside. After their deep conversation about her past during the ride to the restaurant, she was grateful when their dinner conversation remained light. She told him about her upcoming interview and he was thrilled for her.

The meal was delicious. They each started with an

iceberg wedge, smothered in Roquefort dressing and bacon sprinkled on top, minus the blue cheese for Charlie. She followed the salad with filet mignon while Jared had a dry-aged porterhouse. It didn't surprise her there were no prices on her menu. Was she uncomfortable? Yes, but the amazing food overrode her discomfort that she couldn't afford this place on her own. Instead, she devoured everything she could, with gratitude.

She even ate an entire loaded baked potato and Jared grinned. "Eating for two, huh?"

"I'm proud to admit I'd do the same thing if I weren't pregnant. I am not, nor will I ever be, one of those women who eats salads for dinner and says it's her favorite meal."

He nodded in approval. "Good, then you won't mind that I pre-ordered dessert."

As if summoned, the waiter walked in and set down a plate he explained was devil's food cake with whipped ganache, which she was told was glaze and chocolate curls. Curly crunchy pieces of chocolate.

One taste and she was in heaven. It helped that the taste came from Jared's spoon.

He scooped her another piece and she let him feed it to her again. "Mmm. God, that's good."

"Do not make orgasmic sounds when I can't be part of them," he said, his eyes darkening.

"You did not just say that in public."

He let out a low, sexy chuckle. "We aren't in public, and yes. I said it."

They finished dessert and he rose to his feet, pulling out her chair as she stood. Again, no surprise to her, she didn't see the bill and assumed he'd left his credit card when he made the reservation.

Back in the limousine, so stuffed she was bursting out of her pretty dress, she leaned back and turned her head toward him. "Since we're back in the talking zone, does your family know I'm pregnant? Other than Noah and Fallon, I mean." Somehow the limousine had become their intimate sharing space.

He clasped her hand, running his thumb over her wrist. "They all know and they're happy for us."

She glanced at her lap. "Did they judge me? For, you know… oops, she did it again?"

"You didn't *oops* alone, and no one is judging you. Least of all my family."

An unexpected tear fell from her eye and he wiped it with a finger before she could.

"Damn pregnancy hormones," she muttered, embarrassed.

He slid a hand beneath her chin and raised her head so she looked directly at him. Then, his lips met hers.

What started gentle quickly turned hot and intense.

His tongue rubbed against hers, his lips moving against her mouth. She grasped his jacket lapels and pulled him closer, the kiss spiraling out of control. Before she knew it, her legs were on either side of his hips and his hard cock rubbed against her sensitive sex.

She moaned, curling her fingers into the shoulders of his sport coat, wishing it were his skin, and was tempted to remove it. Before she could try, the car came to a stop.

"We're at the hotel," Jared said, his breath warm against her neck.

She drew a deep breath and nodded, climbing off his lap. "Sorry," she muttered.

"I'm not."

She waited for the driver to open the door and help her out. Jared joined her and escorted her to her room.

Once they were outside the door, she turned toward him. "Thank you for a wonderful night."

He brushed her hair off her cheek. "Thank you for joining me."

"Jared, do you want to come in?" She'd thought about nothing else since exiting the limousine, walking through the lobby, taking the elevator to her floor, and now staring into his green eyes.

He braced his palms against her cheeks and tipped his head down. "I was hoping you'd ask."

She turned, key card already in hand, and let them into the room. Housekeeping had been in for turn-down service. She could tell from how clean everything looked in the outer room. Without stopping, she walked into the bedroom and placed her bag on the dresser.

Tonight had been lovely, at times intense, but she'd opened up to Jared in ways she'd never done with anyone else. Just talking about her father was like slicing a vein and though she hadn't told Jared much, she'd explained to him what mattered. Which meant she trusted him enough to sleep with him again.

Aware they were treading on thin ice with their relationship, given they were having a baby, she still couldn't resist.

She pulled her hair back and looked over her shoulder to find him leaning against the wall, looking sexy in his jacket and the white shirt he'd already unbuttoned.

Her panties grew damp at the sight of him. "Unzip me?"

He shrugged off his jacket and his shirt followed, and she couldn't tear her gaze from his sculpted chest lightly sprinkled with dark hair.

He stepped closer and unzipped her dress, his fingers trailing along her spine as he eased it down as far as it would go. His determined touch, his warm body heat so close, had her body vibrating with need, her nipples puckering against the flimsy lace bra she wore.

He slid the dress down her body, the garment pooling at her feet. Stepping out, she kicked it aside and pivoted to face him. His heated stare told her all she needed to know. Of course, if she'd looked down sooner, his rigid erection would have let her know the same thing.

He reached out and deftly unhooked her front-clasp bra and when she shook the undergarment down her arms, he cupped her breasts, palming them in his big hands. She glanced down and noticed the contrast between his tanned hand against her pale flesh. Before she could process the sight, he rolled her nipples between his thumbs and forefingers and she couldn't think at all.

Pleasure suffused her, taking control of her body until her knees nearly buckled. He caught her around the waist and lifted her into his arms. He liked to play and she expected him to lift her up and toss her on the mattress. Instead, he was so gentle the sweetness brought a lump to her throat. He was being careful because she was pregnant and though she understood, she liked his gruffer ways in bed.

"I won't break, you know, and neither will the baby. Stop thinking so hard," she said, propping herself up on her elbows.

"Okay then." He hooked his fingers in her panties and pulled them down, leaving her naked on the bed.

He rose and rid himself of his pants and boxer briefs, his thick erection standing upright and ready. Grasping his cock, he gripped and pumped his hand up and down, a drop of precum coating the tip.

He put one knee on the bed and climbed on. "Spread your legs," he said in that gruff, commanding tone that turned her on. Wetness oozed out of her as she complied.

He climbed over her and positioned his cock at her entrance and without waiting, thrust into her. He filled her so she felt him everywhere and he began to pound into her hard, giving her no reprieve.

Nor did she want one.

She loved the feeling of him inside her, sparking every nerve ending and immediately causing her to climb toward a fast orgasm. She'd asked him not to go easy on her and he wasn't. But he knew exactly how to make her come.

Grasping her hands, he drew them up and over her head, not allowing her to hold on to anything as he continued to drive into her. She squeezed her inner muscles around him and he groaned at the sensation. So she did it again.

"You're a tease," he said.

"I'm doing my best," she told him, then bent her

knees and dug her feet into the mattress, hoping it prevented her from falling headfirst off the end of the bed. Not that she thought he'd let her.

The movement of her legs shifted their hips and suddenly he hit her G-spot with every thrust. Pleasure consumed her, causing her to soar, losing track of time and place. From far away she heard a low groan as Jared came right after her.

Her heart pounded in her chest as she tried to catch her breath.

He rolled off her, staying close.

"When I said I wouldn't break, I didn't mean to test me," she managed to say, a light laugh escaping her lips.

"You gave me permission to let go. I didn't hurt you, did I?" He sounded concerned and rolled to his side, propping his head up with one hand.

She reached out and rubbed the worry lines between his brows. "Of course not. That was incredible."

"It was, wasn't it?" he asked with a grin.

She'd already lowered her arms and now stretched them again over her head.

Taking her off guard, he placed his hand on her belly. "It's really happening," he said, as if in awe.

She covered his hand with hers. "It really is. I hope you and I get along as well as I do with Noah."

"Our relationship is not going to be anything like

yours and Noah's."

"What?"

"It's going to be better because we have feelings for each other. No panicking," he said before she could do just that.

She looked into his perfect face, his expression calm, no stress in sight. "Jared—"

"Nope. Let's go shower." From his firm tone of voice, she knew she wouldn't get him to talk about this anymore.

But she wasn't about to forget what he'd said.

JARED KEPT CHARLOTTE too busy to talk last night and she'd passed out from physical exhaustion before she could question him about his *having feelings* comment. The words had just come out and he didn't want to give her time to decipher them any more than she'd wanted to hear them. Sex had been the perfect distraction.

Charlotte was in the main area of the suite prepping the coffee machine and making him a cup before he needed to leave for home, to shower and get to work. He walked in from the bedroom wearing his suit pants and shirt from last night just as the hotel phone rang.

Charlotte picked up the receiver. "Hello?" She listened, then said, "Oh! Sure! Send him up!" she said, excitement in her voice.

"Who's the visitor?" he asked.

She turned toward him, a cup of coffee in hand. "My brother, Dan. I left him a message the other day and gave him my new address and the hotel info. Listen, he's not like me." She handed him the cup. "He works as a delivery guy unless he's out of work because he's been fired. But deep down, he's a good person. He just... drops out of touch too often. I haven't seen him since I've been back," she explained quickly, because her brother was on his way up.

He took a sip of his coffee, dark, no sugar, the way he'd told her he liked it, and the doorbell rang.

Obviously excited, she rushed out of the room to greet her sibling. He put his coffee cup on the counter and followed at a slower pace. She skidded to a stop in her socks and opened the door.

"Dan!" she exclaimed as she opened the door, and a gaunt-looking man walked in, taking Jared off guard. He wore ripped, old pants and a faded T-shirt and looked as if he hadn't slept in days.

"Are you okay?" Charlotte asked him, pulling him into a hug.

He patted her briefly on the back and stepped away. "Fine."

"Well, come in. Dan, this is Jared Sterling. Jared, my brother, Dan."

Jared extended his hand and the other man gave him a limp-wrist tug. "Yeah, hi."

"Come sit so we can catch up! Do you want coffee?"

Jared stepped up beside her. "I think he's jittery enough," he said, whispering in her ear.

She stiffened but gave him a curt nod. "How about water?" she offered her brother, who was looking around the expansive suite she'd booked so the twins had room when they stayed over.

He shook his head. "Nah. Nice digs, though." He nodded as he checked out the view.

"Did you get my new address I texted you? I'll be moving in soon."

Dan nodded. "Swanky address. How many bedrooms?" he asked, his eyes lit with interest.

"F… Three," she said, changing the truth.

Jared knew enough to go along. "But the girls use them and if they share one, the other is Charlotte's office." He didn't want this strung-out man to get any ideas of moving in. In fact, he didn't want him anywhere near Charlotte or the girls. Obviously, she'd decided the same thing and didn't mention the extra bedroom if the girls shared theirs.

Dan ran a hand through his clearly unwashed hair.

"Charlotte, huh? Are you fancy now, Charlie?" he asked, gesturing around the apartment.

She shook her head, her shoulders drooping. "Jared just likes my full name."

She was deflating with every negative insinuation out of his mouth. "We were just getting ready for the day. What are you doing here so early?"

He shifted from foot to foot. "I need a couple of Benjamins and I figured you wouldn't mind helping out your brother."

"You need money," she said, her voice suddenly dull. "Don't you have a job?"

"I got laid off. You know how it is. Bosses who don't understand I got other obligations."

She shook her head. "You mean you don't understand the idea of being punctual or someone relying on you."

"No. Besides, I owe people."

"Dammit!" Stomping into the bedroom, she quickly returned with her purse. She dug through the small bag and came up with her wallet, pulling out the bills inside. "Here. I went to the bank yesterday. This is all I have. Don't come back for more."

"You're the best, Charlie."

Jared glared at the man. "Read the room!" He turned her brother around to face him. "Your sister was excited to have you come visit but instead of talking or asking her how she is after not seeing her for God knows how long, you come to grub money."

Dan turned and snatched the money out of her hand. "Who is this loser, Charlie? Never mind. I don't care. Thanks, sis." He started for the exit and Charlotte let him go.

The door slammed closed behind him.

Face flushed, she spun to face him. "Well, that was humiliating."

He reached out a hand and touched her warm cheek. "You aren't responsible for your brother's behavior. But, Charlotte, you can't keep bailing him out." He shoved his hands into his pockets. "He probably owes dangerous people money and I don't want that blowback on you!"

Her eyes grew wide at his loud tone.

He'd raised his voice and caught himself immediately. "Sorry. It's just, the last time someone lost their mind thanks to drugs, my mother was killed. And I don't want the same thing to happen to you."

She met his gaze and extended her hand. He clasped his palm in hers. "Let's sit and talk."

He nodded and she led him to the couch where they settled side by side. He knew he was about to tell her the most painful part of his life. The one he pretended he'd gotten over but instead he'd just pushed to the back of his mind.

But if he could share with anyone, it was Charlotte.

Chapter Eleven

C HARLIE TOOK JARED'S hand in hers. "I know your mom died. How old were you?"

"Thirteen. Dad was on a business trip. Aiden and I were at sleepaway camp. Dex was at football camp. Fallon was home sleeping, and Remy was supposed to have dinner with Mom. There was a girl he liked and he blew off hanging out with our mother."

"So she was basically alone in the house?"

He nodded. "And one of my father's clients who'd lost a shit ton of money because he refused to take valid advice to sell, broke in and killed her to get back at Dad."

Charlotte gasped. "That's awful! I'm so sorry." She squeezed his hand.

"I tell myself I'm fine, that I don't have any residual emotional scars, but seeing your brother was triggering. The man who killed my mom got hooked on meds after he lost everything. When he couldn't get more benzos, he went to the street for drugs. He was high when he broke in."

He ran a shaking hand over his face and it wasn't a trembling one like her brother's. No, she hadn't missed that Dan was high, either.

"Dan isn't okay and I don't want him anywhere near you, the baby, or the twins."

She opened then closed her mouth again. On the one hand, she completely understood where his concern was coming from. On the other... Dan was the only family she had in her life. "I wouldn't let him near the girls. Ever. As for me, my brother wouldn't hurt me."

Jared's frown turned into a fierce scowl. "But the men he owes money to would."

She shivered at the prospect, acknowledging Jared had a point. But she was more concerned about his emotional torment. And she didn't want his past to cause him pain because her brother brought back bad memories.

She sought to reassure him. "Then I guess it's a good thing I'm in a building with a doorman."

He blew out a breath and nodded. "It's a start. Promise me you won't give Dan full access? That he will have to call up each time he comes by and you can make a decision if seeing him is wise?"

"I promise," she said, meeting his gaze. "And I'll be careful. Dan usually shows up for money and disappears again for long periods of time. I'm the one who keeps hoping he'll change. That he'll come by just to see me or get sober and care about the girls."

"Who he didn't even ask about. He doesn't know you're pregnant?"

She shook her head. "There's never been time to tell him."

"Because it's always about him," Jared muttered.

"I know." She dipped her head in acknowledgment. "I'm sorry this was all triggering for you."

"It's fine. I'm more worried about you."

She leaned over and pressed her lips briefly to his. "Don't be. I've got the situation under control."

Nodding, he seemed to accept her at her word.

He placed his hand on the arm of the sofa, prepared to stand. "I hate to say this, but I need to get going. I have to stop home to shower and change for work."

"Go on. Thank you again for last night." Her body lit up at the memory of his hands on her skin, his cock inside her, and all the ways he took her hard and fast, leaving her completely satisfied.

"My pleasure," he said, his voice gruff, and she sensed he was thinking about the same thing.

IT TOOK A while for Jared to shake off the effects of the morning. He took a hot shower and drank two cups of coffee before hitting work.

He walked into his office to find Brooke there waiting for him, an amused smirk on her face. Meeting his gaze, she tapped her Apple Watch. "Thirty minutes late, Mr. Sterling. That's completely unlike you, so what gives?"

"You're grinning like you already have the answer," he said to the woman he'd moved up to vice president status at the company. It wasn't her place to question his hours but she was talking as his friend, not his employee.

She sat on the edge of his desk while he unpacked his laptop and water bottle. "Well, you're not the type of guy to spend all night with a woman during the week. Work is too important. On the other hand, you're going to be a father and you have an obvious interest in your baby's mother."

He raised an eyebrow, grateful for the ability to stop thinking about the events of this morning. "How would you know that?"

She shrugged. "I know you well. If you weren't into Charlie, you'd be a lot more shaken up by the idea of being a father."

"Do you want to talk about what really happened between you and Aiden that makes things so awkward now?"

"Not really," she said, her cheeks turning a healthy shade of red. "And touché." She grinned at his non-subtle way of making his point. Good thing she wasn't sensitive and understood him.

Both she and Aiden avoided all discussion about each other and their past, leaving Jared damned curious. Knowing he wouldn't get answers, he focused on his own life.

And considering he'd just spent all night with Charlotte, and he'd admitted out loud that he had feelings for her, and this morning he'd felt completely protective, he wanted to sit with those feelings, and not discuss them. Not even with Brooke, who was like a sister to him.

"On another subject, did you see the invitation to the gala next weekend? I left it on your desk yesterday as a reminder." She glanced at the desk where he'd piled stacks of papers before heading out yesterday. "I guess not," she muttered.

"I didn't need the invitation to remember the gala that's in honor of my mother."

After Gloria Sterling died, once his father pulled himself together, he'd set up a charity to help fund drug programs for addicts. His mother's killer—they never said his name—had been on benzos at the time of the murder and his attorney's argument was that in his right mind, he'd never have hurt Gloria Sterling.

No one in the family knew whether that was true but the need to help people was obvious. And anything they could do to keep their mother's name alive was important.

Jared was notorious for ignoring galas unless he had no choice. Give money? He was all in. Attend an event? Not if he could avoid it. Too many people, too many single women looking for a man with money and, worse, too many mothers looking to pair up their daughters. But next weekend, his whole family would attend and Jared wouldn't miss it.

"Why don't you invite Charlie?" Brooke suggested, waggling her eyebrows.

He shook his head at her antics and laughed. "That might be the best idea you've had all morning."

"It's the only idea I've had since we haven't gotten down to business yet." She tucked a strand of hair behind her ear, picked up her iPad, and took a seat, ready to work.

An hour later, they'd wrapped up their meeting and Brooke headed to her own office. Before making any business calls, Jared pulled up Charlotte's name and hit call.

She answered on the second ring. "Hi, Jared."

"Hello, beautiful. I'm calling to ask you to accompany me to a gala next Saturday night. Black tie," he said.

"A gala?"

He leaned in his chair and pushed back, propping

his feet on his desk. "It comes with the territory. This one's in honor of my mother. The money goes to programs for drug addiction. I go but it's always difficult. And it would be much more pleasurable with you at my side."

"That's a cause I can get behind," she murmured. "I'm sorry all these things are back-to-back. My brother, the gala…"

He shook his head. "I'm fine. I just want to spend time with you."

She let out a light tinkling of laughter that made him smile. "Well, aren't you the charmer."

"I try." He grinned. "So? Next Saturday night? I should warn you, my family will be there and there's no time like the present to make a statement."

"What kind of statement?" she asked, wariness in her tone.

Clearing this throat, he said, "That we're a team, you and I."

"Jared Sterling, are you avoiding the word *couple* because you think I'd freak out?"

"The thought had crossed my mind."

"Well, you'll be happy to know I agree. We *should* make a statement. We're raising our baby together and sometimes… we're—"

"You can say it," he urged. "A couple."

And if he had his way it would be more than

sometimes, both in reality and in her mind. One step at a time, though. She'd agreed to go with him.

"It's just…" She paused. "I don't have another black-tie dress," she said softly. "Just the one I wore to the wedding and since everyone who saw me is going to be there…"

"Don't worry about it. I promise you'll be set."

"What do you mean?"

"You'll see. Thanks for agreeing to be my date. So, when are you moving in?"

She groaned, obviously not looking forward to the prospect. "I spent the morning on the phone with moving companies. How is Friday?"

He nodded. "That works. I'll make the arrangements for you with the building supervisor and take the day off."

"Oh! I know how important work is to you. I can handle the move by myself."

He shook his head, realizing how little she knew him, but he'd rectify that. Make sure she knew she could rely on him. Since Friday was days away, he'd give her some space. He'd be living above her and seeing her daily soon enough.

CHARLIE WOKE UP the day after Jared invited her to

the gala, showered and readied for the day. Her plan was to go shopping for a dress that was appropriate for a black-tie affair but wouldn't break the bank. Tomorrow she'd be out of the hotel and she could begin to regulate her spending. The girls were coming over after school to spend the weekend, help unpack their bedroom, and get used to the new apartment. She was excited to get them settled into the new place.

A knock sounded on her door and she opened it to find a bellman standing with a dolly filled with garment bags hanging from the high bar. "Delivery for you, Ms. Kendall."

"I didn't order…" Her voice trailed off as she took in the name of a very expensive department store on the bags and she immediately knew.

What had Jared done?

"Come in," she said, and rushed to her wallet to pull out a tip which she handed to the man once he'd settled the dolly in a corner of the front room.

"Thank you," he said, and left her alone with what she assumed was a selection of gowns.

She bit the inside of her cheek as she pulled down one zipper to find a silver beaded gown with ruching along the stomach. The second bag had a teal Grecian gown with one shoulder knotted at the top. And the third was a simple black trapeze-style gown that obviously had some give around the waist.

Knowing she shouldn't but unable to resist, she looked at the tag on the silver one, gasping at the price. She glanced at the shoe boxes on the bottom, caught sight of the name, knew they had red soles, and tried not to pass out. How he knew her size was beyond her but she had a feeling her girls might have played a role. They'd always liked to try on her clothes and no doubt they had an idea of sizing.

The allowance around her bump was a no-brainer. She was going to have to buy a size up in leggings soon. After the twins, this second pregnancy had her body changing shape very quickly.

She ought to scold him for spending so much but she couldn't. Not when he'd been so generous and he really wanted her to come with him.

A card stuck out of one of the shoeboxes and she pulled it out, opening the envelope and reading the note inside. *Keep them all. No doubt you'll look beautiful whatever you choose. I'm sure there will be other galas and events for us to attend. Jared X*

"Oh wow." She'd assumed she'd choose one dress and he'd call to have the others picked up once she'd decided.

This whole moment was like a dream, she thought, twirling in the mirror. Except it wasn't. This moment and these garments were real. Which meant she needed to keep a smart head on her shoulders and remember this wasn't some fairy tale.

Jared was her baby's father, a man she enjoyed spending intimate time with, but he wasn't her Prince Charming. Even if this exorbitant gift said otherwise. Keeping her wits about her and her heart to herself was the only way she'd survive this situation. Because they were tied for life by their baby and she couldn't risk rocking that boat.

Knowing which gown she preferred, she tried on the silver, praying it would fit. Though she couldn't zip it herself, she could tell the size was right, as was the silhouette. She looked like an elegant woman who just might belong at the event, especially when she'd put on one of the three pairs of Louboutins, something she never thought she'd own.

Blowing out a breath, she called downstairs and made an appointment at the salon for the works next Saturday, knowing nothing less than her very best would do. Jared deserved to walk into the event with someone who'd put effort into her appearance. Though she might pretend she fit in, at least she'd look the part.

As she slipped out of the dress and hung it back up, she noticed a small shopping bag across the dolly from the shoes. Inside she found a silver handbag that would go with all the gowns but was especially perfect for the one she'd chosen.

When she was finished trying on the other two dresses—just in case—and finding they all looked beautiful on her, she repackaged the shoes and the handbag and placed them on the dolly. Everything would be ruined if she tried to stuff it in the small closet.

Once back in her normal old clothes, she picked up her phone and she noticed her hands were shaking and her heart was racing inside her chest. No one had ever treated her so well or made her feel so special. She might want to protect her heart and her emotions so she could continue to be her non-reliant, independent self… but Jared was making it very difficult.

She called Jared, reaching his voicemail. She left a message filled with all the excitement and gratitude flowing through her at the moment. He deserved nothing less.

After the exertion of trying on the gowns, she was ready for a nap. A quick look at her phone before she closed her eyes and she discovered an email from the museum who'd requested an interview. They offered a few dates and times to meet. Charlie gave them the order of her preference and between Jared's gift and the interview, it was a wonder the adrenaline flowing through her body let her sleep.

She woke up to a voicemail from the twins, both yelling for their turn to talk, but Dakota asking her if she wanted to go for a pizza dinner with Noah and Fallon. She called and replied with a definite yes. She enjoyed the company and the meal, so grateful to be home with her daughters.

Thursday, she packed up her hotel room and settled her account, doing a pre-checkout at the front desk. She napped in between gathering her clothing, cosmetics, and toiletries. The gowns were still in their garment bags and she'd have to make sure the driver was careful transporting them to her new home.

Jared called a few times, never letting her forget he was a part of her life now. More than once she had to calm her hormones that surfaced when she heard his deep voice and the way he—and only he—called her Charlotte. Tingles went through her body every time he said her full name. He even dialed her from the office late Thursday night. Knowing he was working late so he could be with her for the move tomorrow touched her deeply.

She tossed and turned that night, anticipation of her new life keeping her awake. So did thoughts of living below Jared, knowing he was so close, and remembering how he'd played her body perfectly.

She'd even had to unpack her vibrator and give herself an orgasm, all the while pretending it was Jared's talented tongue on her clit while she came.

When it came to the man, she was in deep trouble and she hadn't even moved in yet.

Chapter Twelve

C HARLIE MET THE movers at the storage facility
where she'd kept her furniture and other things
while she was away. After they loaded up the truck,
she headed to her new apartment where Jared was
waiting to give her the keys and be there while the
men unloaded the boxes and placed the pieces of
furniture where she directed them.

Once the movers left, they ordered in sandwiches
for lunch, ate, and then began to dig into the boxes,
starting with the girls' room. It was more important to
her that they be comfortable than taking care of any
other section of the apartment. Jared didn't allow her
to lift anything and was at her beck and call.

She'd continued to unpack their things when the
doorbell rang. Surprised, she looked at Jared. "Who
could be here?" she asked.

He shrugged but she thought she caught the edges
of his mouth lifting up in a grin.

Since he rose to his feet and walked out to answer,
she continued her job. Dakota's dinosaurs, those she
hadn't taken with her to her dad's, went on a standing
bookshelf along with her favorite books and other

things. Next came Dylan's coloring supplies, which went on one side of the double desk she'd bought for them, and her favorite stuffed animals on different shelves.

The sound of voices drifted toward her and she rose to her feet. Curious, she walked into the main room where she was startled to see much of Jared's family had gathered.

"What is everyone doing here?" she asked, surprised.

Noah stepped forward, Fallon by his side. "We thought you'd need help unpacking so... here we are. Put us to good use." He gestured around at the various family members. From Alex, who she knew no one would let help, to Lizzie, then Raven and Remy, and Dex and his wife, Samantha. The only ones missing were Aiden, who was abroad, and Brooke, who Jared explained was holding down the fort at the office.

A lump rose to her throat as she took in all these people willing to help her. Her hand went to her chest as she fought back tears and tried to find the words to convey her appreciation. She didn't have a big family. Her brother didn't think of her unless he needed money, which left her with no one to speak of, and this group was a lot—in all the best ways.

"Thank you," she finally managed to say. "I'm just so overwhelmed. I—"

"No thanks necessary," Jared's father said, stepping toward her. "Welcome to the family." He extended his arms and she stepped into his friendly embrace, feeling awkward and yet so very grateful.

When Alex stepped back, Charlie's thoughts scattered, as Lizzie spoke next. "I'd be happy to get the kitchen unpacked if you point out the boxes," she said. "You can always rearrange things to your liking later."

Though Charlie wanted to tell everyone she could handle the unpacking herself, that was the independent Charlie talking. The more rational part of her knew she'd been nauseous since she woke up; she was already exhausted and had barely begun working on the girls' room.

"I had the movers put the boxes in each room by their labels. All the kitchen supplies should be in there already. Thank you. I can't express how helpful this is and how appreciative I am."

Fallon walked over and slung an arm over her shoulders. "Everyone needs help once in a while. It's not a bad thing to accept it. How about I direct everyone else where to go and what to do, then we can get the twins' linen out and—"

"Raven or Samantha will make the beds," Jared said, gesturing between Charlie and Fallon. "You two don't need to be stretching and overreaching."

"I was about to say the same thing," Noah said.

Fallon rolled her eyes at her husband. "To quote Dakota, did you know in the olden days, women had babies and went back to work in the fields right after?"

Charlie covered her mouth with one hand. "She didn't say that."

"On the way home from dinner last night," Fallon confirmed. "Noah was instructing me on what I was and wasn't allowed to do here today. Dakota chimed in."

Shaking her head, Charlie couldn't hold the laughter in any longer. "Oh my God, that girl." She burst out laughing.

"Gotta love her," Noah said, grinning. "Not that her educational comment changes what you two ladies will be doing today."

Knowing the men were just looking out for them, Charlie opted not to argue and Fallon did the same.

The rest of the day passed quickly, every couple choosing a room and unpacking. By the time the twins were due home from a friend's, whose mom had offered to drop them off, Charlie's gratitude had become mixed with exhaustion and relief.

The unpacking was finished and the family had gone home. Though Charlie had offered to bring in dinner for everyone, no one wanted to put her out. Lizzie thought she should spend the first night in her new place with her girls and everyone else agreed.

Except Jared. He'd remained.

Charlie was with the twins in their bedroom, each sitting on their own bed, the painting they'd made with Fallon hanging on the wall beside them.

"How do you like the new apartment?" she asked them.

"So. Cool," Dylan said.

"Totally cool," Dakota added. They looked at each other and had one of their silent conversations where Charlie was excluded and they talked without speaking. "But we want pink walls."

"Can we, Mom, please?"

She opened then closed her mouth again. She hadn't even considered painting the white walls.

"What color pink?" Jared asked, joining them.

"Light pink!" they exclaimed at the same time.

Thank goodness for agreement. There wouldn't be an argument about color tone.

"Listen, I have an interview on Monday but since I'm not working, I could paint—"

"No." Jared stood, arms crossed above his chest, and shook his head.

"What?" Charlie was used to doing what she wanted and what she thought was right for herself and the twins.

The girls looked from one adult to the other.

"I'll get the room painted." He tipped his head to-

143

ward the doorway.

She took the hint. He wanted to talk. "Be right back," she said to the twins, and followed him into the hallway. Meeting his gaze, she stated her case. "Jared, it's my apartment, my girls want their room pink, and I want to paint it."

"What about the fact that you're pregnant?" he asked in a low voice in deference to the fact that she hadn't told the twins.

She was offended by the implication she wouldn't think about carrying a baby and keeping it healthy. "I'd use water-based paint. I'm not reckless or stupid!"

"No one said you were. But if I can have it done for you and the girls, I want to. Maybe it'll help them warm up to me."

"They like you plenty," she said.

"But they don't really know me. And they need to get used to me being around."

She bit down on her lower lip, then said, "For the baby."

He opened his mouth to speak, when Dakota's voice interrupted them.

"I'm hungry!"

"One minute!" Charlie called back.

Jared tipped her head up with his finger. "This discussion isn't over. Also, when are you going to tell them?"

She swallowed hard. "I talked to Noah. I wasn't sure if he felt he'd want to be there for them. But he said it's my call. I can explain it to them when I'm ready."

"Do you want to do it together?" he offered.

She blinked in surprise. "You'd want to do that? Help me tell my girls?"

He took her hand in his. "How many times do I need to tell you? We're in this together."

She met his gaze, everything inside her pleased by his words. After a day of having help and being catered to, she was in an emotional state and this sealed it. "I'm not used to this. People wanting to help me, being surrounded by family who cares."

"By a man who cares?"

"Mommy!"

"Coming, girls." Squeezing his hand, she sent him an apologetic look. "We can pick this up later."

She turned and walked into the bedroom, focusing on the girls and dinner and not the sexy man who stayed for the meal.

Chapter Thirteen

IT WAS JARED'S first time out alone with the twins. He'd volunteered to take them to the paint store to choose the color they wanted for their bedroom. He'd asked Charlotte to come but also explained he wanted to get to know the girls better. She was only too happy to let him and he promised to send a picture of the chosen color to her for approval before buying.

Then, she'd wished him luck.

He picked them up from Charlotte's apartment and they headed out. They stopped for pizza and he was now sitting across from the girls, who were wearing *different* shades of pink, which he was sure didn't bode well for agreeing on color. Especially since he'd ordered a pizza with half pepperoni and half plain after bickering over the toppings each girl wanted.

"So, are you girls excited to pick your room color?" he asked.

They nodded, eyes wide.

Dakota, her hair in a ponytail, put down her half-eaten slice. "Did you know Elvis Presley had a pink Cadillac?"

"What's a Cadillac?" Dylan asked, wrinkling her

nose in confusion.

He smiled. "It's a type of car. Back when Elvis had it, the car was much bigger and longer than cars today."

"I want Elvis car pink," Dakota said.

He bit the inside of his cheek so he wouldn't laugh. Not when she was so serious. "We'll see what shades they have that you two agree on."

He picked up a pepperoni-laden slice and took a bite just as Dakota asked, "Are you gonna marry our mom?"

He choked on his pizza and grabbed a sip of his soda to wash it down.

Dylan pushed her plate back and folded her arms on the table as she met his gaze, obviously also wanting an answer. Put on the spot by two ten-year-olds. "I think it's a little soon for that conversation."

"So you like her, not love her?" Dakota asked. As if that was the simple reason in her mind.

He met their serious gazes. "I like your mother a lot." He was falling for her more every day, in fact. Not that these two needed to know that.

She nodded. "I saw you put your hand on her back like Daddy does with Fallon."

Aah. That made more sense. He'd have to be even more discreet in the future so the girls didn't get ideas Charlotte wasn't ready for.

He debated on the best way to answer and finally decided. "Well, I want to get to know your mom and you girls even better. Is that okay with you?"

They tipped their heads to the side in the same manner. "I guess so," Dylan said.

Dakota nodded.

As approval, he'd take it. "Let's finish eating so we can go pick paint!" He deliberately changed the subject, not wanting to be interrogated further.

Once they arrived at the paint store, however, he almost wished he was back at the diner being grilled by them. The salesperson at the store had laid out a bunch of light pink swatches and the girls had narrowed their choices to four colors, which hadn't been easy. Who knew there were so many shades of pink?

"Okay," he said, glancing at the similar-looking samples. "We have Rose Silk, Pleasant Pink, and Touch of Pink for your light pinks." He touched each as he spoke. "And then we have Damask Rose, which is a little deeper and has more color."

"I don't love the really light ones," Dakota, who was known for liking brighter colors, said.

"Okay, but I love Touch of Pink." Dylan pointed to her choice.

"I think I like the Damask Rose."

He chuckled. "Those are both good colors." And they were very different.

"If I may?" the salesperson asked.

He nodded. "Please. Any help would be welcome."

"Girls, what if you do one wall with the Damask Rose? It's a darker color and I think it would make the room feel too small. And the other three walls can be Touch of Pink? That way, both of your choices are included."

He watched them closely. Dakota tapped one finger on her color but remained silent, obviously thinking. Since he'd been a kid once, he assumed she was adding up the three light pink walls to her one.

"You could ask your mom if you can buy sheets and pillow cases in your color, Dakota. That would give you more of it."

She nodded. "It would! Good idea!" She smiled, beaming at him, and he felt ten feet tall.

"Dylan? Is that okay with you?" he asked.

She nodded with a smile. "I like the compromise. That's what Mommy says we have to do. Compromise."

"Your mommy's very smart. And so are you two. Okay, let's take pictures to show her, and can we take the color swatches with us?" he asked the saleswoman.

"Of course. I can also paint color samples on paper so you can hang them up on the walls to see how they look."

After the photos were snapped, the saleswoman

handed off the paint colors to a colleague to do what she'd promised.

"Can we FaceTime Mommy?" Dakota asked.

He nodded, opening his phone and pulling up Charlotte's contact. "Go ahead." He handed Dylan the phone.

They talked to their mom and after a few minutes of chatter and happy squeals, Dakota said, "Mommy wants to talk to you."

He took the phone and turned it toward him. Charlotte was grinning as she said, "Hi."

"Hi, yourself."

"Rough day?" The smile turned into a laugh.

He shook his head. "Not at all. They were perfect angels." And for ten-year-olds, bickering was normal.

"I wouldn't think less of you if you told me the truth. But I'm so glad you took them. They seem happy."

"They're experts in the art of compromise, thanks to you."

She nodded. "First thing you learn as a mother of two, especially twins. Well, if you like the samples, I can buy the paint now or you can wait and hang them on the wall to see? I trust you and the girls. If they're happy, I'm happy." She looked down and moved off screen, obviously distracted for a moment before popping back on again. "I can give you my credit card number and—"

"No. It's on me, and before you argue, call it a landlord's prerogative to have the walls painted for his tenants."

She sighed but he watched as her expression changed and she gave in. "Thank you. I'll make it up to you."

"No, you won't. The pleasure of your girls' company is all I need. I'm serious. They're great kids." Who were talking while he'd taken a few steps away to speak to their mother.

She put a hand to her chest. "I think so too, but I'm biased. And so happy to be back home where I can see them all the time."

He loved the warm expression on her face when she mentioned her girls. Wanted to see more of that when she was with him.

"I think we should tell them about the baby when you bring them home," she said.

He drew a deep breath. More inquisition, he thought, surprised he was actually looking forward to it. "See you later, Charlotte." He heard the gruff rumble in his tone only she brought out in him.

She blushed, telling him she'd heard it too. "Bye, Jared."

He disconnected the call and walked over to finish up with the twins, the paint, and take them home.

When they arrived at Charlotte's apartment, she wasn't home from running an errand, so he let them in with the key she'd given him in case of such a contingency. The girls went to hang up paint colors on the walls and he settled in a chair in the living room, exhausted. And for a man who worked the hours he did, that was saying something.

Charlotte arrived soon after and with a quick wave, she went straight to the girls' bedroom to ooh and aah over their choice. A little while later, they walked out, the girls quiet.

"What is it, Mommy? What do you want to talk to us about?" Dylan asked.

"Come sit." She strode to the sofa and sat, then patted either side of her.

As the girls settled in, she shot him an easy smile, letting him know she wasn't panicked about it. He relaxed but not much.

"So, Jared and I have news."

"Good news or bad news?" Dakota tucked her legs beneath her.

"We think it's good news," Jared said.

Charlotte took each of their hands. "I'm pregnant and you're going to be big sisters."

It was as if a bomb dropped in the room. Silence descended and his anxiety ramped up high. He'd come to like the girls; they were sweet and kind and their bickering reminded Jared of him and his brothers growing up.

"A baby? Cool!" Dylan said after processing so long Jared was worried she was upset, angry, hurt.

"Wow," Dakota chimed in. "Boy or girl?"

Jared's gaze came to hers and he tipped his head. It was her choice if she wanted to find out the sex of the baby now or when he or she was born.

"We don't know yet. And I think we'll wait and see. Surprises are good, right?"

They were bouncing in their seats.

"Yes!" Dakota exclaimed.

"Surprises are cool!" Dylan added.

Dylan swiveled, pinning him with her smart stare. "I knew you liked my mom." She wrinkled her nose. "Mommy, how are babies made?"

Charlotte's eyes opened wide.

"When a man and a woman like each other, they get in bed and—" Charlotte covered her other, more precocious daughter's mouth with her hand. "We can discuss this another time. When we're alone," she said pointedly, then cautiously and slowly removed her hand.

To Jared's mortification, he felt his cheeks flame. Life with these girls was going to be very interesting.

He took the elevator to his apartment, needing a drink, a hot shower, and sleep. In that order. Telling the twins he and their mom were having a baby had been… interesting, to say the least. They'd both been happy. But when Dylan asked how babies were made, he thought he was going to choke. Charlotte had turned red and though she'd promised to explain another time, she no doubt hoped her daughter would forget the question.

Not a chance in hell, Jared thought. Dakota was like an elephant. She forgot nothing. And if Dylan didn't bring it up again, her twin would. But he was relieved they'd both accepted he'd be around more and as he'd gotten ready to leave, Dakota pronounced him Daddy Jared. Because he was the baby's daddy, she'd explained.

Despite her reasoning, the name affected him on an emotional level. This little family called to him in ways he still didn't understand.

Chapter Fourteen

THE REST OF the weekend was exceptionally busy with him playing catchup with work obligations. Still, he'd tried to stop by Charlotte's apartment as much as he could and she seemed to understand work was pulling at him. Which made her different than any of the other women who'd passed through his life.

He appreciated her good-natured acceptance of his job, though he'd assured her things would lighten up when Aiden came home and helped him out.

He came by on Monday morning, fixing up punch list type items in the apartment, then he decided to stop by his father's house after work.

After seeing the twins' room filled with stuffed animals and other items important to them, he had the idea of going home. The basement was full of things from all his siblings, labeled by kid and pressure-sealed in boxes. He wanted to see what was in his mementos from childhood and what he could pick up for his kid.

His kid.

The thought was still surreal.

Not for the first time, he wished his mom were here to meet her first grandchild. A lump swelled in his throat and he swallowed over it, pushing it down.

After he arrived, he spent some time with Lizzie who was cleaning up from dinner, then headed to his dad's home office to visit before he hit up the basement.

He knocked once and walked inside. To find his father smoking with the window wide-open, puffing smoke out the screen.

"Goddammit, Dad!"

"Jared! What are you doing here?" Alex rose from his seat, the cigar dangling between two fingers.

"Never mind that. What are you doing with that thing in your mouth? Again? The doctors told you to cut that shit out for good. I've been working my ass off to keep you healthy and you're still sneaking around behind my back?"

To Alex's credit, he dipped his head in shame. "I quit. I swear. And then when we had that problem with Randalls and the scandal and plunging stock. I took one puff to relax... and I was hooked again. It's hard."

Jared snapped. "You know what's hard? Me, working my ass off to take your place so you stay healthy. Me, giving up a life, dating, women, to dedicate myself to this business so I can take over from you one day and make you proud because I'll never know if I could have made Mom proud."

Now, where the fuck had that come from? He shook his head, attempting to dislodge the thought from his brain.

"Oh, son." Alex stubbed out the cigar, rose from his seat, walked toward him, and slung an arm around his neck. "Your mother loved you. She loved all of you and you all make her proud." He drew a breath. "But especially you," he said in a gruff voice. "Because you're taking care of me."

He didn't know how his father knew but… "I needed to hear that. And I need you to quit smoking and drinking. And coming to work too early and staying too late." He paused, then admitted, "Because I can't lose you, too."

His father's face crumbled, tears in the older man's eyes. "I never thought of things that way, through my kids' eyes." He dipped his head. "Okay. I finally hear you."

"I hope so dad, because I love you. We all do."

Father and son hugged it out and Jared pulled himself back together emotionally. Clearing his throat, he said, "I came here to go to the basement. I wanted to look through my old boxes of stuff."

His dad nodded. "Want me to join you?"

Jared shook his head. "I'll be down there awhile."

He left his father and walked the hall leading to the basement, then down the long flight of stairs. His father had the walkout finished when they moved here and he knew exactly where to go. In the large square closet with white shelving sat the labeled boxes.

He pulled down the one he remembered looking through as a kid and opened the sealed top. He sorted through comic books and baseball cards, baseball trophies, a mitt, and other various objects he remembered from his childhood. He could definitely give his boy... or girl a mitt and teach them to throw and catch.

He lifted a piece of cardboard and underneath was the one thing he never admitted to anyone that he'd kept. Only his mom knew his secret. A light green stuffed alligator with little white teeth.

"Chester!" he said aloud and let out a loud laugh.

He'd kept the stuffed animal hidden beneath the covers when he was little and never let his siblings see. If any of his brothers had known he couldn't sleep without it, he'd never hear the end of it.

He didn't know how old he was when he'd parted ways with Chester, but his mother had kept him. And boy or girl, Jared would be passing it on to his child.

After he gave the thing a good washing.

He packed up the box again, knowing he'd be back as the baby grew, grabbed the alligator, and left the basement, suddenly needing to see Charlotte. She'd understand the emotional turmoil his father put him through and he needed her.

He texted, letting her know he wanted to stop by and she gave him the okay. She was starting to feel less tired, she'd told him, and felt able to stay awake a little later.

So, he headed over to see his girl. Even if she wasn't ready to accept the proprietary feelings he had for her, he felt them nonetheless.

CHARLIE SET HER phone on the counter, surprised Jared had asked if he could come over to talk. He stopped by often but something about his request tipped her off to his distress.

She took a quick shower and dried her hair. Since she'd had the girls last week, Noah had them this week and she'd been in bed reading. Or trying to read. She'd had the interview at the museum today and it had gone exceptionally well. So well, that the woman in charge had offered her the position immediately, saying she was afraid of losing Charlie if they waited to talk to other candidates. Charlie didn't tell her there was no one else banging down her door.

She did, however, mention her pregnancy. To her relief, it hadn't been an issue and she'd accepted on the spot. She had a job and no one to tell. Leo was out of town for work. Her instinct had been to call Jared, but she knew how busy he was at the office and didn't want to bother him. Or come to think of him as someone she could call to share news. It scared her, how much she wanted to rely on him.

By the time she'd finished getting ready, it was time for Jared to arrive. She put on a long, silk robe and waited. Despite knowing he was coming over, when the knock sounded on her door, she jumped, startled.

She pulled in a deep breath and walked over to let him in. She opened the door to find him looking more vulnerable than she'd ever seen him. His eyes were sad, she thought, and those lines furrowed between his brows.

"Hi," she said softly. "Come on in."

He stepped inside. "Hey." His gaze dragged over her, lingering on her chest.

She glanced down at the low V she hadn't realized had formed at the lapels of her robe, and knew she was blushing. "I took a shower before you got here. No makeup…" No clothes. What had she been thinking?

That she was comfortable around him, that's what.

He chuckled. "You look beautiful with or without makeup."

"Thank you," she murmured. "Are you okay?"

Not only did she want the focus off herself, she desperately wanted to know what was bothering him.

"Not really." He ran a hand through his hair, then walked through the apartment and sat down on the sofa.

Instead of settling beside him, she plopped down on the stone cocktail table, their knees touching, and waited for him to explain.

"I went to see my father tonight and caught him smoking. I let him have it."

She rubbed her hands on the soft material of her robe. "I'm sure he understood."

He nodded. "He did once I explained I just wanted him to be proud of me because I didn't know if my mother was."

Her mouth parted in a silent O. "Jared," she whispered. "You're such a good, kind man. A solid one. You work hard and make sure your father doesn't have to. You take care of the people in your life." And she realized how lucky she was to be one of those people.

Not breaking eye contact, she continued. "You've stood up for me since the minute I told you I was pregnant. I couldn't ask for a better father for my baby." She took his hands and squeezed. "And if I know one thing for sure, it's that your mother is *so* proud of you," she assured him.

"That's what my father said."

"He's right." She was so touched he was sharing this hard truth with her, exposing his vulnerability. He was so strong and he didn't even realize it.

He reached into his jacket pocket and pulled out something green.

"What is that?" she asked.

He set what she realized was a stuffed animal on her lap. An adorable alligator with little hands and flat white teeth. "Oh my gosh. Where did you get it?"

He chuckled. "Not it. Chester. That's his name." He went on to explain he'd picked him up from his box of childhood things at home. How he'd hid him from his brothers, and the only one he'd trusted was his mother.

"I brought him home for our baby's room. When we get it set up, I mean."

She glanced at his matted fur and kept silent on the condition. "That's so sweet." She picked up Chester and held him to her chest. "I love that you thought to bring something that meant so much to you."

Keeping his gaze on hers, he took the alligator from her hands and put him on the table, then leaned forward and sealed his lips over hers. He slid his tongue into her mouth and rubbed against hers, arousing her until her nipples poked against the silk of her robe.

As if he knew, he reached down and squeezed her nipples between his thumbs and forefingers, making her writhe on the table. She hoped she wasn't leaving a wet spot.

Again, he read her mind and broke the kiss, then rose to his feet. He scooped her up so she was clinging to him like a spider monkey, her legs around his waist, her arms around his neck. Resting her face against his cheek, she inhaled his masculine, sexy scent, wriggling against him so her clit got friction from his hard erection pushing against the fly of his pants.

"Mmm. Jared, I really need to come."

He let out a gruff chuckle. "Oh, I intend to make you come, beautiful. Again and again."

"Promise?"

He lay her down on the bed, untied her robe, and parted the sides. "You're naked."

"No, I have a thong on. It's nude."

A tug on one side and he ripped the panties off her body.

Once she truly was naked, he came down over her sex and dragged his tongue through her pussy. Her hips jerked and she pushed herself against his mouth. Taking the hint, he licked up one side and down the other, sucking her flesh into his mouth and nibbling with his teeth.

She squirmed against him, seeking pressure on her

clit, but he focused everywhere but where she needed the friction most. She pulsed with desire and emptiness until he slid his tongue inside her and pressed hard on her clit with his fingertip, rubbing persistently. Waves of bliss wafted through her and she arched her hips, riding the surge until she came apart, kneading her sex against his mouth until her climax ended and she dropped, sated, onto the bed.

"Are you ready for me? Or do you need a minute?" he asked, as he rose to his feet and stripped off his clothes.

She might be tired but her pussy still throbbed with desire. "I need you to fill me."

"And I want to see you come again."

She giggled and said, "Not sure you saw me the first time."

"I beg to differ." He raised an eyebrow. "I think I had the best view."

Her face heated with embarrassment. Before she could focus on that comment, he placed one knee on the bed and climbed over her, his cock poised at her entrance. Without warning, he pressed in all the way. Not fast and hard, but gentle, his gaze never leaving hers.

Every shift and glide in and out was filled with emotion, scaring her as much as it pulled her in like a rapid current. She was falling for him in a way she'd never experienced before. The emotions swirling through her were new and frightening, but she couldn't stop them from working their way through her and settling, a heavy feeling in her chest. One she recognized as a deep connection.

He shifted his hips and the sensations grew more intense, her body soaring higher and searching for something just out of reach.

"Jared!" she cried as she dug her nails into his back.

He picked up the rhythm, thrusting harder, his long, thick cock hitting her in just the right spot, over and over, and her orgasm slammed into her. She let herself go and soared until the waves receded and she wrapped her arms around him, holding on while he found his release.

A little while later, she lay cuddled in his arms, thinking about how close they'd become in such a short time. Tonight, he'd confided in her about his childhood and close bond with his mother. She'd already let him in with so much about hers. She couldn't deny or fight the truth but she could try to hold on to that sense of self-reliance she had.

Being hurt by her father or her brother was bad enough, but if Jared did anything to sever the fragile bond they'd built she didn't want to be in an emotional place where she'd crumble. She could be stronger than that. Still, she felt safe, happy, and content in his arms.

"How did your interview go today?" he asked. "I wanted to call but every time I picked up the phone, someone needed me for something."

At the reminder, she experienced a lurch of excitement. "I got the job!" She told him how well she'd meshed with the interviewer and how impressed they'd been with her employment history.

"Congratulations! Not that I had any doubt." He squeezed her tight and she leaned back into his embrace.

"Thank you. I'm excited."

"I am sure you'll do a phenomenal job."

His faith in her wrapped around her like a warm blanket and she cherished the new sensation and allowed herself to revel in the amazing feeling of Jared being proud of her.

She was well aware she wasn't the only one affected by tonight's lovemaking. She couldn't call it anything else. She'd seen the warmth and feeling in his eyes when he was deep inside her and decided to immerse herself in it.

For now.

Chapter Fifteen

THE WEEK FLEW by and suddenly the day of the gala arrived. Though it had been her week with the twins, Noah had their steady Saturday night babysitter watch them for the evening. Once Noah and Fallon officially became a couple, then married, the twins stopped their antics of driving away sitters, and accepted Greta, a young woman who Fallon met and hired. A Swedish student on a work visa, Dakota pumped her for information about her homeland and Dylan just liked her fun personality.

Charlie spent the day pampering herself. She couldn't say she was used to it but by the time she walked out of the salon, her hair pinned up for the night, her nails done, and her face fully made up, once again she felt like a different woman. One she was getting used to seeing in the mirror.

She arrived back home to change and wait for Jared to pick her up when she saw a man huddled in the corner of the lobby, his hands in his jacket pockets and his shoulders hunched over.

She looked at the brown hair and immediately knew. "Dan?"

Her brother turned to face her and she gasped at the black eye he was sporting. He limped toward her, showing her his bruised lip.

"Oh, Danny," she said, using his childhood nickname. "What happened?" She reached to touch his face and he flinched, backing away.

"I walked into a door?" He laughed awkwardly at his horrible joke, as he shifted from foot to foot.

She frowned. "That's not funny. Seriously, are you okay?"

He nodded, lying. "Yeah, yeah, I'm fine."

She narrowed her gaze, not believing a word he said. "What *really* happened?"

"None of your goddamn business!" he said, his voice rising.

Wincing, she glanced at the doorman witnessing the scene.

"Ms. Kendall, do you need me to have him removed?" the young man asked.

She cringed inside and shook her head. "No thanks, Kevin. Everything is okay."

His frown told her he didn't buy it. She wasn't sure she believed her claim, either.

She turned back to her sibling. "If you're okay, then why are you here? What do you want?" she snapped at him. "I have somewhere I need to be."

His expression turned into a sneer. "Yeah, I can

see you're all high and mighty now." He gestured to her made-up face and coiffed hair. "Which means you have money to lend your brother."

If only he knew. She hadn't started her job, not until Monday, and wouldn't be paid for two weeks. She was living frugally when she didn't have the girls to worry about.

"I don't have any cash on me," she told him. She'd used her spare money for tips.

He sighed. "Come on, Charlie, please?"

Her heart split in two at his plea. "Is it drugs?" Because he was definitely jittery.

He glanced from side to side, making sure no one was around or listening. The doorman was busy with his cell phone. "It's not drugs, exactly."

"What does *that* mean? Are you clean?"

Refusing to meet her gaze, he swung his head back and forth. "No. But that's not it. It's the guys I've been hanging out with. They did something… bad. And because of that, they got me into trouble."

Typical Dan, never taking responsibility himself. "God, Danny."

His eyes filled with tears, his expression tight but also wide with fear. She couldn't imagine what kind of trouble he was in to have such an extreme reaction.

Finally, he let out a pained sigh. "Never mind. I'll figure something else out," he muttered. "Just worry about your own life. I'll be fine."

She hated the guilt trip but she'd bailed him out too often. At some point, he had to stand on his own. This was the time. She couldn't have anything to do with the kind of problems he was having.

"I'll always worry about you. You're my brother. But you need to get clean, face the consequences of your actions, and start to fix your life."

Knowing she shouldn't, she opened her bag and found the few twenties she had left, shoving them into his hand.

"Thanks, Charlie. I know I need to fix things. I just don't know how."

She squeezed his shoulder. "Figure it out."

Taking her by surprise, he leaned forward and kissed her cheek. "Thanks, sis."

She watched as he limped away and slowly headed up to her apartment to get ready for her evening. Though how she'd enjoy it now, she had no idea.

JARED SAT IN the back of the limo with the most gorgeous woman he'd ever laid eyes on. His sister's stylist had outdone herself with the silver gown and Charlotte had added to the look by having her hair and makeup professionally done.

He appreciated both the everyday woman and this more elegant one and he was touched she'd went to the effort again. But instead of her sparkling eyes matching her glowing skin, she had a distant look, as if she were somewhere else, not here with him.

He slid his hand over hers. "Charlotte?" When she didn't answer right away, he repeated her name, tapping the top of her hand with his fingertips.

She startled then turned toward him. "Oh! Sorry. What did you say?"

"I was trying to get your attention. Where are you?" he asked.

She sighed. "I had a visit from my brother. He was waiting in the lobby when I got home this afternoon and he'd been beaten up." Her eyes shimmered with tears.

She pulled a tissue from her purse and dabbed at them. "Dan told me that he and the guys he hangs out with are in trouble. I sensed it was beyond owing someone money, though that's his usual MO."

Jared frowned, and opened his mouth to lecture her about her brother and his so-called *friends*, but caught himself in time. Charlotte was upset. She didn't need him adding to things by scolding her about having anything to do with her sibling. Especially when he couldn't imagine turning his back on his brothers or sister. The fact that her brother triggered his worst fears wasn't her issue; it was his.

"I'm sorry," he said, the words lame but the best he could offer. "Was he high?"

She nodded.

He drew a deep breath and let it out again. "You know, if he ever wants to get clean, I can get him into a good treatment center. I'd be happy to pay for it and with the connections through tonight's charity, it would be one of the best in the country."

"Jared. That's beyond generous. I wish he'd take you up on it." She shook her head as if no was a definite answer.

"Well, the offer is always open."

She met his gaze, her first smile of the night lighting up her face. "Thank you. And thank you again for this." She waved her hand up and down the glittering silver gown.

"My pleasure. Especially since I get to look at you in it all night." He reached into his pocket and came out with a long box. "This is for you."

Her eyes, surrounded by thick, black lashes, opened wide.

"You didn't have to get me anything. In fact, you shouldn't have."

Ignoring the comment, he popped open the box.

She glanced down and gasped at the tennis necklace he'd bought. All diamonds except…

"The two pink sapphires are for the twins. And the jeweler said he can add a blue sapphire or another pink one after we know the sex of our baby."

She gasped. "Oh my God. This is stunning. It's too—"

"Don't say too much. Turn."

She pivoted so he could wrap the necklace around her bare neck and do the clasp. She spun back to face him. "I'm speechless. It's so beautiful and meaningful. I never expected you to buy me anything, let alone… this." She touched the full set of diamonds surrounding her neck.

"It's not as beautiful as you. You're giving me something I never dreamed of having for myself. A baby. A family."

Leaning in, she pressed a kiss to his lips. "Don't worry, it's stainproof." She laughed and shook her head. "Thank you seems so insufficient."

The car drew to a stop and cut off the discussion about the necklace. "We're here. Are you ready to go in?" he asked.

"I am."

The driver opened the door and after Jared climbed out, he helped Charlotte, wrapping an arm around her waist as he led her inside.

CHARLIE SAT BY Jared's side at the family table, listening to the formalities of the event. They all welcomed her warmly and she felt like she belonged, a feeling she was still getting used to.

Samantha, who she hadn't spent much time with, walked over, joined by Raven. "Who wishes they were home in sweats watching television?" Raven asked.

Charlie laughed at the comment. "Normally I would, but this is my first time in such an amazing gown and shoes—" She swept her arm up and down her body. "I'm enjoying dressing up tonight."

Samantha nodded in agreement. "I like the occasional glam night."

Raven sighed. "Okay, just me then." The women went on to talk about things in their lives, including Charlie in the conversation, which she appreciated.

A tapping sound echoed around the room and when she looked over, a woman was standing at the microphone.

"Oops. That's our cue to sit down." Samantha touched Charlie's arm. "I look forward to getting to know you more," she said.

"Same here." Raven smiled, and Charlie took her seat.

Jared settled in beside her. "Is everything okay?" he asked.

She nodded, smiling. "Your sisters-in-law are

great," she said.

He slid his hand into hers. "I'm glad they're making you feel welcome."

The woman at the podium began to speak.

Charlie's hand touched the necklace at her throat and she let her mind wander. Not to her brother, who she couldn't do anything to help if he wasn't ready to accept her help, but to Jared, and his generosity. Of course, the necklace was sparkling and spectacular and she'd never owned anything so beautiful. But the thought behind it…

And that he'd included the twins. Girls that weren't his own. He hadn't just been thinking about the baby they'd share but her daughters, too. There was no better way to win her over than to care about her girls and make them an important part of his life, as well. The best thing about Jared was there was no calculation in doing so. He truly cared. This man was breaking down her walls more with each passing day.

Her thoughts were distracted when Alex rose from his seat to a round of applause. Standing at the podium, she listened to him talk about his deceased wife and how she would still be here today if not for a man addicted to drugs, who'd gotten access to a gun, and killed her in the name of revenge.

At one point during the speech, he winced and lifted his hand to his chest and Jared nearly bolted out of his seat, as did his siblings, but he finished without incident.

She squeezed Jared's hand and held on for the duration of Alex's speech, which impacted all the Sterling siblings sitting around the table. Lizzie dabbed at her eyes and Charlie found a new respect for the woman who gave Alex a second chance at happiness.

He returned to his chair and reassured his family he was fine, but from Jared's tight jaw, he was skeptical. He'd even whispered his worry in her ear but he was forced to take his father at his word.

Later, with the night winding down, Charlie danced with Jared, his strong arms wrapped around her waist. She inhaled his sensual cologne and her body sparked with need. His stiff erection rubbed against her as he moved, the desire between them equal and obvious.

"This reminds me of when we spent time together at Fallon and Noah's wedding," she said.

He chuckled in her ear, the sound low and deep. "As if I'd forget."

She smiled as they slow danced to the music. Aroused but also safe and content in his embrace.

"This might be too forward," he said. "But do you want to get out of here?"

Hearing the exact same phrase he'd spoken to her that same night, she smiled. "I don't have a room upstairs this time but yes, I'd love to."

"My place or yours?" he asked.

The girls were sleeping at their dad's, so she didn't have to worry about them after the sitter left. "Surprise me."

He checked in with his father. The twins were fine. Then they said their goodbyes and walked out, hand in hand. Jared said something to the driver and they headed home in comfortable silence, her head on his shoulder.

They pulled up in front of his building and she followed him inside where she spent a glorious night in his bed.

CHARLOTTE WOKE TO the sound of a cell phone she recognized as Jared's. Checking the time on her cell, she realized it was too late for a normal call. Still, she really needed to go to the bathroom, so she rushed out of bed while Jared answered the phone.

She returned to find he was out of bed and pulling on his pants. "What's wrong?" she asked, rushing over to him.

"That was Remy. My dad's in the hospital and it's serious." He ran a shaking hand through his hair. "We all knew something was wrong tonight. Why did I let him talk me into buying he was fine?"

She pulled him into a brief hug. "Let me get dressed and I'll come with you." She didn't want him to be alone.

He buttoned his shirt, not bothering to tuck it in. "I should tell you to stay in bed. To get some sleep, but I really want you by my side."

She was relieved to hear his answer. "That's good because you couldn't talk me into staying here and sending you there alone."

He shot her a look of gratitude, and they finished dressing then rushed to the hospital to be there for his father.

Chapter Sixteen

J ARED MADE IT to the hospital in his car in record time. With his entire family gathered in the waiting room, there was no space for anyone else, but it was past midnight and the area was empty, except for them. There was also no room to pace, which left everyone huddled in small groups.

Despite the fact that he'd talked with his father after yelling at him for not taking care of himself, Jared was torn. On the one hand, he'd been right or they wouldn't be in the hospital now. On the other, he felt guilty for yelling at his dad and now he was being taken care of by doctors who wouldn't let anyone in to see him.

He and Charlotte had switched places with Remy and Raven, taking their seats while they walked over to Dex and Samantha. Fallon was with Brooke and Lizzie, while Noah stayed home with the girls.

Charlotte slipped her hand into his. "What are you thinking?" she asked.

"That I wish I hadn't had an argument with my father about him not taking care of himself at the same time knowing I was right."

She squeezed his hand. "He knows you have his best interest at heart."

They sat that way for another few minutes when Remy walked over.

Charlotte rose to her feet. "I'm going to take coffee orders and go to the machine. It's the best I can do at this hour. Can I get either of you anything?"

"Black," they both said at once.

She nodded.

"Thanks, Charlie," Remy said.

Jared treated her to a warm smile. "Thank you."

She nodded and walked off to take more orders.

Remy lowered himself into the now empty seat beside Jared. "Dad's tough. He's going to be okay." He put a hand on Jared's back.

"Also stubborn. Whatever this is, he's going to have to start following doctor's orders if he wants to see his grandchildren grow up," Jared said.

Remy nodded. "Agreed. Maybe tonight will scare him enough to do just that."

With a shrug, Jared said, "I had this argument with him a few nights ago and a few weeks before that. I feel guilty as hell about yelling at him, but he needed to hear it."

"You did the right thing."

"The Sterling family?" A doctor with salt-and-pepper hair asked as he stepped into the room.

Everyone turned and the man's eyes widened. "Okay then. I'm Dr. Vitale, the cardiologist called in to see Mr. Sterling."

"How is he?" Remy asked.

"Stable," the doctor said.

There were audible gasps of relief. Brooke put an arm around her mother, and behind the doctor, Charlotte had walked into the room with a tray holding quite a few paper cups of coffee.

Jared strode over while the doctor spoke, took the tray from her and placed it on a table. Then he stood beside her.

"So due to those two blocked arteries, I'd like to operate and do bypass surgery on them, especially with one of the arteries being the main one. They're clogged and we need to get them open and the blood flowing."

Jared shuddered at the thought of his father having open-heart surgery.

"Can we see him before?" Fallon asked, her voice shaky.

The doctor nodded. "He's being monitored overnight and we won't operate until tomorrow. But two at a time, and please keep him calm."

Once the doctor left, the family agreed on Fallon and Lizzie going in first. As long as Jared saw his father, he didn't care what order he went in.

One thing he knew for certain, he wouldn't have gotten through this ordeal as well as he had without Charlotte by his side.

Turning to face her, he braced his hands on her hips. No one in the room paid attention to them, everyone focused on Alex and their own feelings in the moment.

"You've been my rock," he told her.

She smiled and stroked his cheek. "I'm glad I could be here for you."

"No, you don't get it. You're the reason I haven't crumbled under the pressure of waiting to hear if I was going to lose another parent. Not my siblings, *you.*"

She parted her lips but didn't speak. That was okay. He had enough to say for both of them. "I never had anyone who cared enough to be there for me and I didn't give enough of myself to do the same for someone else. You did that for me. You stood by my side, and I'd do the same for you."

"I've never had that either." Tears filled her eyes but they weren't sad ones, he knew by the small trembling smile trying to break through.

Fallon and Lizzie returned to the room and everyone pivoted toward them. "He's doing well," Fallon said in a shaky voice. "Remy and Dex can go in next."

Jared would go afterward as they'd agreed on chronological order except for Fallon and Lizzie. If

Aiden had been here, he'd go in with Jared.

He'd left a message for his sibling and Jared hoped he'd call back soon.

Twenty minutes or so later, Jared's turn came. He followed a nurse's directions and strode down a hallway until he came to his father's room.

He knocked once and walked in.

His dad turned toward the door. His face looked pale, small oxygen tubing wrapped around his face and up his nose, and his smile was forced. "Hi, son. Come on in."

A chair was already pulled up to the bedside and Jared sat down. "How are you feeling?"

"Like a stupid old man."

Jared shook his head. "Don't be so hard on yourself. It's hard to admit when you have to slow down."

"I didn't follow doctor's orders. I fought with my kids. I smoked, ate like shit, and thought I was tough enough, that I knew better. I ignored all the warning signs, and now I'm facing heart surgery."

Jared covered his father's hand with his, leaning on top of the waffled blanket. "You are tough, Dad, and that's why you're going to get through this." Jared wasn't upset with his father. It had to be hard to face his own mortality. "I felt guilty after our argument, but you know I'm just looking out for you, right?"

His dad nodded. "I was wrong. With all my kids.

With Lizzie." His face looked more lined than before and there was definite regret in his eyes.

A lump rose to Jared's throat. "I love you, Dad. You're going to get through this."

"Damn right I am," his father said.

And when Jared left, he was smiling.

Chapter Seventeen

A FEW WEEKS passed after Alex Sterling's heart attack. He had done well during surgery. Better yet, he'd learned his lesson about taking care of himself. He'd stepped down at Sterling Investments, turning the title of CEO, the highest role, over to Jared.

And since Aiden would return for good next month, Jared had insisted he be named CFO. He'd explained to Charlie that he didn't want feelings of resentment festering once Aiden learned the ropes, after he studied for and took his Series exams. Brooke, too, had been promoted to COO, chief operating officer.

During the time that passed, Charlie adjusted to full-time work and she loved her new job. From shadowing the resident docents so she learned everything about the museum, to prepping to give guide tours herself, to cataloguing new items, she enjoyed both the work and the people. The staff included her during lunch hour and she'd gotten to know them all well.

Only once had she met Leo for a quick bite to eat,

and Jared had joined them so he could meet her friend. Given how often she spent time alone with Jared in the evenings, she rarely saw Leo, though they texted and talked to catch up. He had met someone he was now dating and they'd both been less available.

Jared, despite wanting to cut back to more normal hours, had still been working late in the evenings, but somehow they'd gotten into a routine of him coming over for dinner, Charlie cooking and waiting for him to eat. As a result, they'd grown closer.

Today, Charlie was leaving work early for her eighteen-week sonogram. She'd gone to her last monthly checkup and had an ultrasound. According to the doctor, it was early and the baby had been shy, not revealing its sex, but the doctor had assured them they'd know at the next appointment.

Despite her saying she'd meet Jared at the obstetrician's, he insisted on coming to the museum and going with her to the office. She checked out with her boss and took the stairs down to the sidewalk on the street level to wait for Jared.

The temperature was in the mid-seventies and a warm breeze blew around her. As usual, the city streets were busy with people walking past in both directions.

A man with a beanie and a green army jacket slowed as he passed, bumping into her. His dress sense was odd for this time of year.

She stepped aside, but he eased closer. "Tell your brother if he talks, he's a dead man and you're next."

Before she could look up at his features, he dipped his head and took off, leaving her with nothing to describe but his clothing.

His warning settled into her bones and she realized Jared was right. Whoever her brother had pissed off was a danger to her, too.

Shaking, she was relieved when Jared pulled up to the curb in his Land Rover SUV, the large, luxury car with plush leather seats that heated her butt and the most comfortable vehicle she'd ever been in. She rushed over and yanked open the passenger door before he could climb out and do it for her.

She'd locked herself inside, leaving Jared staring at her, eyes wide and filled with alarm.

He stretched his arm toward her seat. "What's wrong?" he asked.

She glanced at her shaking hands and repeated what had just occurred. "And after threatening me, he walked off before I could see his features."

"Dammit!" He slammed his hand against the steering wheel. He put the vehicle in park and reached over, hugging her awkwardly due to his seat belt and the center console, but she took comfort in his familiar, always sexy smell and the way he wrapped her in his arms.

"Are you okay?" He settled back in his seat and studied her, as if he could see through her skin to the trauma beneath. And from the way her insides still trembled, maybe he could.

She nodded, twisting her fingers together in her lap.

"Okay. Here's what we're going to do."

She glanced up at him for answers because she hadn't a clue.

He looked at his gold watch, then placed his hand over hers. "We're going to call and reschedule the doctor's appointment. Then we're going to get you a cup of tea to relax you and a muffin for your blood sugar."

She loved how he looked out for her. Despite all her internal warnings, she'd grown used to his bossy but caring nature.

"And then we're going to see Remy," he said.

"Remy? Your brother who owns The Back Door?" she asked.

Jared nodded. "Remy, the former NYC cop and current private investigator, who also happens to co-own the bar. We're going to tell him what's going on and have him find out what your brother has gotten himself involved in. I refuse to have you in danger because Dan is spiraling."

Gratitude wound through her and she swallowed

over the lump in her throat. "Thank you. I don't know what I'd do if I was alone in this."

He squeezed her hands tighter. "You're *not*. And you never will be again."

JARED AND CHARLOTTE sat across from Remy in his office. Pictures of Remy and Raven were on his desk and family photos hung on one wall. On the other side of the desk was Zach's wife's picture and photos of his partner's family on the opposite wall.

Beside him, Charlotte fidgeted in her seat, her nerves obvious.

Remy steepled his fingers in front of him and studied them both. "What's wrong, and I'm asking as your brother? You both look like you're about to jump out of your skin."

Jared covered Charlotte's hand with his. "Her brother got involved in some kind of trouble and she was threatened outside her place of work."

His brother pulled up his iPad and tapped the screen a few times. "Charlie, give me whatever details you have about your brother, starting with his name and age."

"Dan Kendall. Daniel. Thirty-two." She hesitated and Jared squeezed her hand, encouraging her to go on. "He's been in and out of trouble most of his life," she said. "You'll find he has a record. Petty theft, drug possession." She bit down on her lower lip. "He's on drugs. I don't know what kind, where he gets them or what he owes. But he told me this *trouble* goes beyond owing money. And the guy who threatened me said to tell my brother if he talks, he's a dead man. And I'm next." Her voice shook as she repeated the message.

"You've got to find out who Dan's involved with," Jared said.

Remy nodded. "Can you describe the guy?" he asked Charlotte.

"Only what he was wearing. A blue beanie, green army jacket, and jeans. I noticed because it's so warm and he stood out. He bumped into me, talking while he did, and when I looked up he'd moved past me. I never saw his face."

"Was his hair long? Did you see it beyond the hat?"

She closed her eyes, obviously thinking. "Brown," she said. "Long and brown."

He typed in the information and met her gaze. "I'm sorry you're going through this," he said in a kind tone.

"Thank you," she murmured.

He inclined his head. "Now, I can handle the investigative work but given the threat and the fact that you want to live without worry, I'd hire someone to watch over you." His gaze turned to Jared who inwardly winced.

Though Remy had phrased the words delicately, and despite it being exactly what he'd planned on telling Charlotte, Jared waited for the explosion.

"A bodyguard?" Her voice rose. "Someone trailing around after me twenty-four seven?"

Jared placed a calming hand on her arm. "I was thinking more like the times you weren't home for the night." He drew a deep breath. "And when I'm not around to take their place."

"I have a doorman, so I guess that makes sense," she said, thinking things through aloud. "So I'm safe alone in my apartment."

As if he'd count on the unarmed guys downstairs in case someone really wanted to get to her. But he let her work her way through to the conclusion he wanted.

Remy cleared his throat. "Actually, the guys downstairs are just visual preventatives. It's not like someone who wanted to hurt you couldn't get past them."

Her eyes widened and those gorgeous, pouty lips parted. "I'm not safe in my own home? I have kids and… dammit. I can't have them over until this is resolved." Frustrated tears welled in her eyes.

"You could be perfectly safe as long as someone who could handle themselves was with you," Jared said.

Remy drummed his fingers on the desk, his mouth turned upward in a smirk.

His brother either thought Jared was using this situation to get closer to Charlotte or he understood him at her apartment, or vice versa, would accomplish the same thing.

"I sparred with Remy for years." Jared felt confident in his ability to protect himself and Charlotte, at least in hand-to-hand fighting.

She shook her head as if to clear it. "What are you saying? Just spell it out."

He glanced at Remy. "Give us a minute?"

His brother nodded. "Take all the time you need," he said, and strode out of the office, closing the door behind him.

"I agree the girls should stay with Noah and Fallon until this is resolved. You'd have a bodyguard during the day and me at night until your security arrives in the morning to see you to work." He bluntly spelled it out for her. "I won't risk your safety, period."

She rose and paced the small room. "It's not like being with you is a hardship, but I don't want to put you out."

She hadn't shot down the idea out of hand and

that was a good sign. "I honestly don't mind." He stood and walked over to where she looked out the window at the parking lot. "If it makes you feel better, you could stay with me."

Her silence weighed heavy around him, so he picked up on something else she'd said. "Being with me isn't a hardship, huh?"

She turned and met his gaze then, a smile on her face. "No, Mr. Huge Ego, it's not a hardship. I just hate turning our lives upside down because my brother can't get his shit together." She dipped her head and said, "I'm sorry. I know you didn't sign up for this."

He strode over to her and stepped so close, he backed her against the wall beside the window. Lingering notes of her perfume, a warm, sensual scent, reached his nose and his body responded despite the time for arousal being all wrong.

"I signed up for you. And I refuse to risk your safety, so you have a choice. A bodyguard twenty-four seven or me at night. You decide." He drew a deep breath and let it out again. "Besides, it's not like being with you is a hardship either." He grinned and it broke the tension.

"Bossy man," she said, but treated him to the most genuine smile he'd seen since picking her up earlier. Then she reached up and stroked his cheek. "I choose you," she said, repeating his words back to him.

The knot in his stomach eased.

"But I have two conditions." She held up her fingers in a V.

"Name them."

"I stay by you so it's me that has to pack up and be inconvenienced, not you. And we already agreed on this but I don't bring the girls home until I know for sure it's safe."

He nodded, unable to argue with either point. "Done." Before she could respond, he braced his hands on her thickening waist, loving the changes in her body, thanks to their child, dipped his head, and pressed his lips to hers.

She moaned and wrapped her arms around his neck, accepting the kiss. But it was also the fact that she trusted him to keep her safe that did something for him and he deepened the connection. His tongue wound its way around hers, then stroked the inside of her mouth until she was rubbing up against him like a kitten, her body seeking his.

A knock on the door interrupted the moment. "Fuck my brother," he muttered and resumed his assault, but a second knock had her slipping away from him.

He glanced over to find her touching her well-kissed lips. He started for the door and flung it open. "What?" he barked, expecting to see his oldest sibling.

Instead, it was Raven.

Her gaze flew from him to Charlotte, and her cheeks flushed pink at the realization that she'd interrupted. "I just thought I'd see if you or Charlie wanted something to eat." She waved at Charlotte who now stood behind him. "But I think I'm needed at the bar. Let me know if I can get you anything. Bye," she said and was gone in an instant.

Charlotte groaned, burying her face in her hands. "Mortifying," she said once she'd removed them.

"Nothing those two haven't done in here before us," he assured her.

"That is *not* the point!" Her own cheeks were beautifully flushed. "I need to call Noah and explain all this to him," she said on a sigh.

He nodded. "I'll give you some privacy and meet you out front." He leaned over and brushed her lips with his.

When he lifted his head, her eyes were glazed and he grinned. "Hang in there, sweetheart. Nothing will happen to you. You have my word."

While she talked to Noah, he called Alpha Security and arranged for a female bodyguard, hoping that would make Charlotte more comfortable being protected during the day. He'd take over at night. He refused to take her safety for granted.

Chapter Eighteen

O NE WEEK HAD passed since Charlie was threatened on the street by someone her brother was involved with. Thanks to Jared, she had a female bodyguard named Mia with her during the day, and even Charlie had to admit, the other woman did well blending in at the museum so Charlie could work.

She called her brother more than once, hoping she could relay the message from the man Remy still hadn't tracked down. The first couple of times, Dan's phone went straight to voicemail. The last time, she got a message that the line had been disconnected and her stomach clenched in fear. Knowing there was nothing she could do until she heard from him, she did her best to go about her life. She missed her girls but knew that them being safe was the most important thing.

Jared came home early every night, often bringing work with him. He'd make calls from his second bedroom office while Charlie handled dinner. In return for his generosity, she wanted to make his life as easy as possible. He'd been so helpful and easygoing, and she was grateful.

Even she had to admit she was enjoying the routine they'd fallen into, she thought, as she plated the angel hair pasta and meatballs she'd cooked for dinner. The garlic bread and broccoli came next.

Once she had the food on the table, she knocked on Jared's office door and pushed it open as he'd once directed her to do. He wasn't there, so she walked down the hall to the primary bedroom. This time she knocked and waited for him to let her in. She might be sleeping with him at night but she didn't want to treat it like it was her bedroom. It was the only way to remember this was a temporary situation.

Before she could think further, the door swung open and Jared stood before her, naked but for a towel wrapped low on his hips.

"Hi!" he said, greeting her with a relaxed smile. "Just thought I'd shower real quick before dinner."

"And I came to tell you dinner is ready," she said, but she couldn't tear her gaze from those tight abs and light sprinkling of hair disappearing below the towel… which was rising the longer she stared.

He cleared his throat and she shook herself out of her stupor.

"Oh God. Embarrassing."

He winked. "I liked the fact that you were looking. And if you aren't sure about that, just look down again and—"

"I know!" Her voice rose and her cheeks heated with a pretty flush.

"Tell you what? I'm starving, so let me have an appetizer before we eat."

She thought about all the food in the kitchen. "I have garlic bread if you want to eat that first."

He shook his head, then bent at the knee and scooped her into his arms, losing the towel on his way to the bed. "What are you doing? This carrying me around has got to stop. I'm just getting heavier—"

He gently placed her on the bed. "You're perfect," he said, and hooked his fingers into her leggings. He slid them down and off her legs, underwear with them.

Next thing she knew, her legs were propped on his shoulders, his face level with her sex, and he licked straight up, teasing her with the first stroke of his tongue.

Her core clenched and she moaned.

"Louder," he said, sucking on her folds and nibbling on her clit with his teeth.

She rose with every nip and pull, her body soaring, reaching for something greater than her. "Jared!" she screamed as the first wave of her climax hit.

He slid a finger inside her, pumping deep, then added a second. "Oh God!" She bucked against his hand and when he curled those fingers and rubbed, a second pulsing sensation crested and she rode it until she toppled over, breathing in short, choppy inhales and exhales.

"Now, that's what I meant by an appetizer," he said from where he lay on his side, grinning at her, his mussed, wet hair giving him strong sex appeal.

She eased herself up and maneuvered until she was sitting.

"You liked that, did you? Well, now it's my turn." She turned on her side and scooted lower on the mattress so she was eye level with his impressive erection. Her eyes watered just looking at it and her sex pulsed once more.

Gripping his cock in her hand, she ran her grip up and down the elongated shaft, reveling in his loud groan. He always made her come first, satisfied her in all ways, and she couldn't wait to reciprocate.

She slid her tongue around the tip, tasting his salty essence. Then, she took him into her mouth until she nearly gagged, gliding him out and in again, all the while making sure to keep her hand moving. Taking her cues from his grunts and groans, she kept up the momentum even when he arched his hips up and his cock hit the back of her throat.

"So fucking amazing," he said in a guttural tone, one that aroused her and had her empty sex clenching with need again.

Knowing she pleased him gave her a high she'd

never experienced before and she wanted more. She slid a hand down and cupped his balls in her hand, tugging lightly.

"Fuck!" he yelled, wrapping her hair in his hand and tugging. "I'm going to come."

Ignoring his warning, when he stiffened and his climax took hold, she swallowed until he collapsed against the bed.

She sat up and met his gaze. "That was *my* appetizer," she said and grinned.

A few minutes later, he'd regained his strength and hauled them into the shower. After soaping each other up and rinsing off, she put on a T-shirt of his that hung to her knees. He dressed in a pair of gray sweats that reminded her why women appreciated that choice.

Together they ate cold spaghetti and meatballs, laughed over her mortification in Remy's office, and cleaned up the kitchen before turning in for the night.

As she lay in bed, Jared hugged her against him, his hand on her growing belly, and she accepted the fact that she'd fallen in love with this man. It frightened her but all she could do now was hope and pray he lived up to the person he'd shown her so far.

CHARLIE HADN'T BEEN able to shake the feelings

she'd experienced after making love with Jared. The last barrier around her heart had crumbled and knowing that, she needed someone who wasn't emotionally involved to help her through it.

She let Leo into her apartment and they settled onto the sofa to talk.

"Okay, tell me what's wrong," Leo said, his expression filled with concern.

"I'm in love with Jared."

Leo's eyes widened. "That's a huge admission coming from you."

"A frightening one." One she'd fought against, but she was powerless against her own emotions. "I've always let my past define my actions," she explained. "My mom died, she had no control over leaving me. But my father had a choice and it wasn't me. Noah's a great guy but he was never *the one*. Jared's given me no reason to think he's in this for the wrong reasons, but what if I'm misreading the situation?"

"What if that's your fear talking?" Leo asked. "Love is scary for everyone. But if you don't leap, you'll never know all the good things that are waiting for you on the other side."

Valid point, she thought. "Are you speaking from experience?" Her lips twitched as she thought about her friend falling hard.

"I'll tell you that next time. We're talking about

you." Leo, still dressed in a suit since he'd come straight from the office, crossed one leg over his knee. "I think you're strong and can handle whatever happens next, but if not, I suggest you walk away now. It's not fair to Jared for you to lead him on."

She blinked, his words startling her. "What?"

"Think about it from his perspective. He seems to be doing everything right and you still don't want to totally trust him. He deserves better, don't you think?"

She opened her mouth, then closed it again. "I never thought of things that way." Embarrassment creeped in along with the feeling she'd been selfish in her thinking.

He nodded. "I'm a guy. I can see things you can't and look from Jared's point of view."

Something she'd never done.

Leo steepled his fingers and remained silent, obviously thinking. "You know I love you, right?" he asked at last.

She nodded.

"Well, take this in the spirit in which it's intended. Jared is a good, patient man, but even he'll have his limits. In the end, only you can decide which way to go. And…" He paused, obviously hesitating.

"Just say it." She curled her fingers into fists.

"Don't be your own worst enemy, Charlie. Stop letting your past define your present and your future.

Because if you don't start believing in yourself and your own worth, you'll never accept any man in your life. And that would be a damn shame."

Before she could answer, Leo rose to his feet. "I have to go. I'm meeting Lisa for dinner."

Charlie smiled. "I'm so glad you found her. You deserve a good, solid relationship." She hugged Leo and stepped back.

"So do you. Promise me you'll think about what I said?" he asked.

"I will." She had a feeling that's all she'd be considering.

Chapter Nineteen

C HARLIE SAT IN her favorite club chair in Jared's living room, sipping warm vanilla-and-chamomile tea. She sighed, with as much contentment as she could have, living on edge, waiting for something to happen so her life could go back to normal.

She'd given a lot of thought to what Leo had to say and she knew he was right. Besides, if she trusted Jared to keep her safe, she'd already handed him the keys to her heart. She just hadn't told him yet.

Earlier tonight, she'd met with Fallon, Noah, and her girls so she could spend time with them even if they couldn't sleep home yet. Mia had sat at a table beside her the whole time, refusing to join them, keeping an eye out while they ate. Her plans allowed Jared to work late tonight, something she knew he'd needed to do.

She'd arrived home earlier than him and Mia's shift ended before he returned. She promised she'd stay behind her locked and alarmed door and swore to Mia that Jared would be home soon. Mia left and she waited for Jared.

Taking a sip of tea, Charlie thought back to dinner,

her precocious daughters and their behavior.

"Why can't we come home with you, Mommy? We miss you at night." Dylan spoke in a sad voice that broke Charlie's heart and made her want to throttle her brother for somehow involving her in his mess.

"I miss you too, honey. But we explained why."

"Because Uncle Dan is in t-r-o-u-b-l-e," Dakota sing-songed. "And you don't want us around in case he comes over."

It had seemed like the simplest explanation at the time. One that wouldn't frighten the twins by indicating Charlie might be in danger.

"Someone needs to punish him," Dylan said, her tone mulish because she wanted to be with her mom.

"He's a grown-up. Nobody is going to punish him," Noah said. "He just needs to get some help."

Charlie nodded.

Fallon cleared her throat. "Who's finished with their burgers?" she asked. They were eating at everyone's favorite old-fashioned diner.

"Did you know that mother monkeys slap or bite their babies when they're bad? Maybe someone should bite Uncle Dan's—"

Charlie's gaze swung to Noah's, her eyes wide. "Dakota, what do you want for dessert?" she asked, quickly changing the subject while every adult tried not to laugh.

Her cell rang, taking her out of her memory, and she grabbed the phone. The screen said Unknown

Caller.

She took the call and put the phone to her ear. "Hello?"

"Charlie?"

She recognized her brother's throaty whisper. "Dan? Where are you? Why is your phone disconnected? What's going on?" She shouted the questions at him.

"I don't have much time. Just listen. I know I've been a shitty brother and I'm sorry." He sounded winded and scared and her heart began a rapid gallop in her chest.

"Dan? Where are you?"

"I'm in hiding. Those guys caught up with me. They jumped me and beat the shit out of me. I got away but I'm in serious trouble. If you don't see me again, just know I love you."

"Don't hang up!" she shouted. "Daniel Gregory, you tell me where you are now. I'll come get you." She was not going to lose him, too. No matter what he'd done, he was her brother and he sounded like he was giving up, something she refused to accept.

"Absolutely not."

"Then call the police." It was time he faced the consequences of his actions, whatever they were.

"I can't. I don't want to end up in jail."

"What. Did. You. Do?" she asked, rising and pacing back and forth in the family room.

He expelled a harsh, pained breath. "I was the getaway guy in a robbery where the clerk was killed. But I swear I didn't know they'd shoot him! When I found out, I ran."

Oh my God. Her hand rose to her throat, feeling the pulse beating at the base. "Let me come get you." Somehow she'd talk him into turning himself in, but at least he'd be safe behind the alarm in this apartment.

"No!"

"Please, Danny. I won't even get out of the car." The car she didn't have. But she could take a rideshare and call Jared on the way and ask him to meet her. She'd just have the driver wait until Jared arrived. "Just tell me where you are. I can help you."

He hesitated and all she heard was the sound of his heavy breathing. Finally, he said, "Fine." And rattled off an address she memorized.

"Just sit tight. I'm coming."

Her insides shaking, hands trembling, she put the address into her phone. She didn't know the area but was aware enough to realize it wasn't in a safe part of the city, almost near the Bronx.

Tears in her eyes, she dressed quickly, pulling on a pair of leggings and an old sweatshirt she'd brought with her to Jared's.

Jared.

He was going to kill her, she thought, but would just have to worry about that later. She'd text him as soon as she was in the rideshare and ask him to meet her.

After tying her sneakers, she grabbed her phone, set up a rideshare, unset the alarm, and took the elevator down to the lobby. Shaking but determined, she stepped out before the doors fully opened.

She hadn't made it to the entryway when she heard her name. She turned to see Jared striding toward her, his suit rumpled after a full day, briefcase in hand, and his brow furrowed as his gaze locked on her.

"Where are you going? And where's Mia?" he asked, glancing at his watch.

She bit down on her lower lip. "Umm. Her shift ended and I told her it was okay to leave because you'd be back soon and… I swore I wouldn't leave the alarmed apartment. But—"

His eyes widened. "Then what the hell are you doing downstairs and where are you off to alone?"

She'd never been on the receiving end of his angry tone and she didn't like or appreciate it. She did, however, understand it.

"I had every intention of messaging you from the Uber and asking you to meet me. My brother's in trouble," she said, and reiterated what Dan had told her on the phone. "And I can't just leave him sitting, waiting to be found. I need to help him! But I wasn't going to get out of the car until you got there, I swear. Just show up, text him that I'm there, let him get in the vehicle, and we'd leave. And you'd have been there as backup. That's it."

"That's it?"

She nodded.

He ran his hand through his already mussed hair. "That's it, huh? Do you have any idea how much could go wrong with that plan? You're a woman alone, counting on a rideshare driver you don't know to take you to a shitty area of town, while you wait for your drug addict brother who's being hunted by men willing to kill. Jesus, if I hadn't run into you…" He pulled her against him, his arms wrapping tightly around her.

She breathed in his familiar scent and closed her eyes, appreciating that strong hug holding her tight. But in the back of her mind, the clock was still ticking on getting her brother to safety. "Will you go with me?" she asked.

He slowly released his hold, letting her step back. "Any chance you'll let me go instead?"

She shook her head. "He won't get in the car with you."

Jared let out a pained sigh. "The cops?"

She shook her head again, this time harder. "No police."

"Fine." Grasping her hand, he strode over to the desk, handing his briefcase to the doorman. "Lock this up somewhere safe please? I'll pick it up on my way back home.

"Cancel the Uber. I want to be the one behind the wheel," he said, grabbing her hand and heading toward the elevator to the garage where his car was parked.

CHARLOTTE WAS GOING to be the death of him, Jared thought, driving toward the address she'd given him and he'd put into his GPS. He didn't want to make this trip, especially not *with* her in the car, but he knew she'd go whether he accompanied her or not. And the latter wasn't an option.

The deeper he drove into this shitty part of the city, the more his apprehension grew. He wished he'd made Charlotte go back upstairs where he'd have locked her in his apartment. Not that he could have done it, but he sure as hell had wanted to.

He glanced over.

She sat beside him, twisting her hands in her lap and staring out the front window, her anxiety palpable.

"There's still time to change your mind," he said.

"No." The sound came out like a croak but she'd stiffened and refused to budge on her stance.

So he was driving his over one-hundred-grand car into a place they'd strip it if they could. He didn't give a shit about the vehicle, but it also told him how concerned he was bringing his pregnant girlfriend into this part of the city. An Uber would have been less obvious but Jared wouldn't have been in control and he had a feeling he needed to be.

Graffiti lined the buildings, at least from what he could see in the dark, and men hung out on street corners in what he was sure were dangerous gangs. Given what he knew of her brother's issues and now the illegal situation he'd gotten himself into, he wasn't surprised by their surroundings.

Thank God they continued driving past the hang-arounds and finally pulled up on a dilapidated, quiet street with run-down two-story houses.

"Here." Charlotte pointed to a number on a beat-up old mailbox and Jared pulled the SUV to a stop and put the car in park.

He blew out a nervous breath. Though he could handle himself, only an idiot wouldn't be worried.

Thanks to his headlights, he got a better look and realized dilapidated was too kind. The home looked more like it ought to be condemned. Shingles hung off the front, the shrubbery was dead, and even in the semi-dark, thanks to his headlights, it was obvious the paint was chipping.

He turned to Charlotte, whose face was now pale. "Second thoughts?" he asked.

"Yes, but I'm not leaving without my brother."

"Got it. Then you are staying here. Get in the driver's seat in case you need to leave."

She stared at him, horrified. "I'm not leaving you!"

"If it gets dangerous and bullets fly, you sure as hell are. I mean it, Charlotte. I'm not getting out of this car without your promise. You look out for yourself first." Her and their baby.

"Fine."

"Say it."

"I'll leave if it gets dangerous," she said without meeting his gaze.

He shook his head. "Your fingers better not be crossed where I can't see." He drew a deep breath. "Now call or text your brother and tell him to get his ass out here or I'm coming in."

She pressed the buttons on her phone and put the sound on speaker, but the call went straight to voicemail. She texted Dan next and they waited in silence.

He gave the man three minutes and let out a curse. "Text him again that I'm going to get him." She did as he asked. "Now come switch seats with me."

She exited the vehicle and he met her outside his door, helping her in. "Shut the door and lock it," he instructed.

She treated him to a salute but he saw the fear in her eyes. Leaning over, he pressed his lips to hers before slamming the door shut and waiting to hear the click of the lock before starting up the dried-out lawn.

He arrived at the front door only to find it partially open. He was creeped out but pushed the door further open and stepped inside. Looking around, he didn't see anyone and began to make his way through the house, checking in the living room, then the kitchen.

The sound of a crash startled him and he realized it came from upstairs. He slowly made his way up, checking behind him every few steps. At the top of the stairs, he faced a bathroom with the door open a crack.

"Dan?" he called out.

The other man peeked through the opening, his one black eye showing. "Jared? Charlie said you'd come." He flung the door open, revealing white powder all over the old, dark wood countertop.

He had a bruise on his jaw, his lip was split, and he held his side as if his ribs hurt badly.

"I didn't mean it," he said, hopping from foot to foot.

Jared frowned. "We can talk in the car. Let's go." He wanted to get the hell out of this place before whoever was looking for Dan found him.

"I swear, I didn't know they had a gun."

Charlotte had already explained the situation and it was as bad as it could get. "Come on. We're leaving now. Talking later."

Jared stepped closer, grabbed the other man's skinny arm, and all but dragging him down the stairs, around the corner, and out the door, him yelling about how it hurt the entire time.

He didn't give a shit about the man's pain. He wanted to get Charlotte out of here and to safety. This shitty neighborhood was freaking him out. Nothing could happen to her or his baby. Allowing her to come had been a mistake.

They were steps from the car and he caught her wide-eyed gaze when two men approached, seemingly out of nowhere.

"Fuck." Jared glanced at the car and narrowed his gaze, silently warning her not to dare unlock the vehicle. He turned as a hooded man grabbed Dan, one arm around his waist, the other holding a knife to his neck.

Seconds later, Jared was pushed from behind and plastered to the hood of the car, the second man holding him in place. Taken by surprise, he expelled a rough breath of air, aware he had to fight this guy off.

But the only thing going through his mind was Charlotte as he prayed she stayed in the damned car.

★ ★ ★

CHARLIE WATCHED THE house, barely blinking as she waited for Jared to approach the old, run-down home and knock. Her stomach bottomed out when he walked inside and disappeared from sight. Time seemed to slow as seconds, then minutes passed.

When she saw Jared and Dan rush down the grass to the car, she breathed out a sigh of relief. And then two men jumped out of the bushes from the side of the property and she screamed in surprise. In the blink of an eye, her brother had a knife to his throat and Jared was thrown against the hood of the car by a man with a tire iron in his hand.

The guy with the knife pushed Dan forward and looked Charlie in the eye. "Get out of the fucking car."

"No!" Dan screamed.

She couldn't hear Jared but his lips moved and she had no doubt he was warning her to stay put.

She froze, not moving, her heart pounding in her chest. The police, she thought, grabbing her phone from the center console. She had to call the police. Dialing 911, she hit speaker, giving the operator the address where they'd come to get Dan. She prayed they'd arrive soon.

"Did you hear me? Open the door and get the fuck out here!" the same guy yelled, pressing the knife closer to her brother's throat.

"Ouch!" Dan yelled as blood dripped down his neck.

No way was she letting them get hurt if it was in her power to stop it. "Stop!" she screamed before all hell broke loose.

Jared headbutted the man holding him from behind and broke free, the other guy grabbing his bleeding nose. While he was distracted, Jared swung, nailing him in the jaw, then kicked out and got him in the abdomen. Obviously not expecting it, the man fell to his knees.

Charlie was panting, fear overwhelming her, but she trusted Jared to handle things.

Dan tried to wiggle free, but he was trembling and too unsteady. Jared thrust out his foot, nailing the man holding Dan in his knee. He threw her brother to the ground and went for Jared, who appeared ready to take him when the second guy, the one Jared had taken out of the equation, rose to his feet.

Charlie flung open the car door to warn him, screaming as he hit Jared in the back of the head with the tire iron and he fell to the ground, seemingly unconscious. "Jared!"

Both attackers turned her way, taking a step forward, when the blessed sound of sirens filled the air. The men froze, whispered something to each other, then took off at a run.

Charlie fell to her knees by Jared's side. "Jared?" she asked, her hand shaking as blood oozed from the wound in his head. Afraid to move him, she sat by his side, caressing the side of his face. "You'll be okay," she said softly. "You have to be okay."

She glanced up at her brother who was jumping where he stood. "The cops are coming. I have to go!"

"Don't you dare," she hissed. "Jared was hurt because I insisted on rescuing you. You sit down, shut up, and take responsibility for once. You owe him that."

A patrol car screeched to a halt behind the SUV and an officer climbed out, his partner walking around the vehicles beside him.

"He needs an ambulance, now!"

One officer called it in while the other grasped her brother's arm as he tried to slink away.

Fear and nausea warred inside her as she sat waiting for paramedics to arrive, stroking Jared's cheek, saying prayers the entire time.

Chapter Twenty

G UILT SWAMPED CHARLIE as Jared's family piled into the waiting room, a place they were too familiar with even if it was a different hospital. She backed against the wall, hoping nobody sought her out. She didn't know what to say beyond telling them it was her fault Jared was injured.

He'd come to as the ambulance arrived and not only did she refuse to leave his side, he refused to let them transport him in the bus without her. But when they pulled into the emergency room, they'd rushed him inside, leaving her to sit in the waiting room where she called Noah. She asked him through her tears to let the family know, and settled in to wait for word from a doctor.

Noah and Fallon walked in last. They'd needed to get a babysitter before they could come. Though she hated to leave here, Charlie had offered to go home to the girls so Fallon could be here for her brother, along with her husband. Maybe it had been due to the hysteria Charlie couldn't control but Noah insisted she stay put and they'd be there soon.

Before the couple could make their way to her,

Remy strode over and leaned against the wall by her side. "Hey."

"Hi," she said softly. "I'm so sorry."

He cocked an eyebrow. "Did you hit him with the tire iron?" he asked.

She shook her head, her lips lifting in an unwilling semi-smile. "No."

"Then don't apologize. When I met Raven, she was being stalked by her half-brother. If I'd been injured, would it have been her fault?"

Again, she shook her head.

"Nobody blames you," he assured her, astutely getting to the core of her concern. At least her second worry because she was jumping out of her skin not knowing anything about Jared.

She swiped at her eyes. "I called the police as soon as those guys jumped out at them, but it took time for them to get there. The ambulance took even longer. But Jared was awake the last time I saw him."

Remy squeezed her hand. "That's good, honey. Now breathe. If I don't take care of you, my brother is going to kick my ass."

She blew out a long breath. "Where's Raven?" she asked.

"She went to get some coffees."

"That's good. I'm sure everyone can use them."

He nodded. "I wish we'd hear some news about

Jared, though."

Charlie nodded. "I know. I can't take the wait." She looked around, noticing Raven walk in, coffee in to-go trays in her hands. "I'm fine. Go help Raven," she said.

He cocked his head to the side. "Are you sure?"

"Yeah. Thanks for checking on me."

He winked at her. "Anytime."

She glanced up at the ceiling. Brown stains—water marks—told the tale of how old the structure was. Closing her eyes, she forced herself to box breathe, a count of four in, hold for four, and breathing out for four, then repeating the cycle to calm her anxiety.

"Charlie?" Noah said her name.

Her eyes snapped open. "Hey," she said to him and Fallon. Meeting the other woman's gaze wasn't easy. "I'm sorry. He was helping me rescue my brother and… it shouldn't have happened. I—"

Fallon grasped Charlie's hand. "It's not your fault."

Charlie swallowed over the lump in her throat. "That's what Remy said but it sure feels that way."

"I—"

"Jared Sterling's family?" Fallon spun toward the doctor and rushed forward to hear what the man had to say.

Charlie lingered in the back, hoping to hear or have the news repeated to her secondhand.

"There are a lot of you," he said, chuckling.

That had to be a good sign, right? Charlie wondered.

"We ran scans and besides a concussion, there's nothing alarming about the results. We used staples to close the wound. He'll have a nasty headache and some side effects of that but otherwise he'll recover just fine."

Charlie didn't hear anything else he had to say. Her legs began to shake and dizziness assaulted her. Spots floated in front of her eyes and she recognized the signs. She was going out. A glance told her the nearest chair was too far, so she tugged on Noah's sleeve and lowered herself to the floor, putting her head between her knees.

"Jesus." Noah bent down and she heard the rest of the family's chatter, but all she could do was breathe and think, *thank God.*

Jared was going to be okay.

JARED LOVED HIS family but if one more sibling walked in—he'd seen his father, then his brothers with their wives—he was going to scream.

Remy and Raven strode in after Fallon and Noah left, and Jared narrowed his gaze. "Nothing personal, but where the fuck is Charlotte?" he asked.

Raven inclined her head. "You tell him," she said.

Remy stepped forward. "Charlie insisted the family come in first. Believe me, we tried to convince her otherwise, but she feels guilty and doesn't want anyone upset with her. Or, to quote her words, more upset with her—though nobody's mad. Everyone understands the situation."

"Do me a favor?" Jared asked. "One of you go get her?"

Raven smiled. "I'll do it. They're enforcing the 'two at a time' rule. Remy, stay with your brother. I'll be in the waiting room with your father and Lizzie. Everyone else has seen you and gone home."

Once Raven had left, Remy pulled up a chair, sat down, and leaned forward. "I also think Charlie's feeling out of place without you."

Jared knew better than to nod, add to that shake his head or move much, because the pain was excruciating. The doctor had ordered a pain killer he didn't want to take until he'd seen Charlotte. Then he'd be happy passing out since they insisted on keeping him overnight for observation.

Charlotte's feelings didn't surprise him. She wasn't used to having a family who cared. People who, once they included you, never let you go no matter what happened.

A light knock on the door had him turning his head. Catching sight of her dark hair, he did his best not to wince. The last thing she needed to see was how much pain he was in.

"Come on in, sweetheart."

Charlotte tentatively stepped inside and Remy rose from his seat. "I'm going to get going. Raven and I need to get back to the bar." He shot Jared a meaningful look. He was leaving to give them time alone.

"Thanks for coming."

Remy patted his shoulder, obviously aware of what a concussion felt like, and said goodbye, then added, "I'll make sure your car is taken care of," Remy assured him.

"Thanks, Bro."

With an incline of his head, Remy walked out and Jared turned his attention to Charlotte.

"Sit down," Jared said in as strong a voice as he could manage.

She did as he asked. "Jared, I am so—"

"Don't say it. Don't be sorry. Shit happens in life. I'm just relieved I'm the one who was hit over the head and not you. If you'd gotten out of the car, I don't know what I'd have done. So please stop apologizing."

"Okay."

"Now slide in closer."

She lifted herself and dragged the chair nearer to the bed.

"Did the police get the guys?" he asked.

She nodded. "Another squad car saw them running from the scene. And they took my brother in, too." Her eyes grew glassy and sad. "I'm honestly glad. He needs help and he's not going to get it at a luxury detox place. He has to face the consequences of his actions and addiction, and if it means getting clean behind bars, so be it."

He doubted it was as easy for her as she made it out to be. She was protecting him because of his injury when he wanted to be the one to look out for her.

"I changed my mind. I want you right here." He slid over, ignoring the pain in his head that throbbed and stabbed like a son of a bitch, and patted the mattress.

Her eyes grew wide. "Jared, don't move. I could see how much that hurt."

Guess he hadn't hidden it as well as he thought. "Okay, but still, come lay with me."

She did as he asked, carefully climbing in and stretching out next to him, and resting her head on his arm closest to her. Her body heat warmed him and every muscle relaxed. Even the pain was manageable with her so close.

He had everything he needed within touching distance. Closing his eyes, he savored the scent of her hair and let himself drift off.

JARED WOKE UP to debilitating pain and Charlotte was gone. He rang the buzzer. The nurse walked in, the promised medication in hand, she just hadn't woken him to administer it. A first for a hospital, he was sure.

According to her, the shift before her had insisted Charlotte leave when visiting hours were over.

He was pissed, knowing how many walls she could construct around her while he lay here incapacitated. Not happening, he thought.

He was getting out of here tomorrow.

WHEN THE NURSE told Charlie it was time to leave because visiting hours were over, instead of packing up and returning to her apartment, she went home to Jared's. She called her girls, promising to bring them home to their new place tomorrow. Then, she took a warm bath, letting the water soothe her aching body. Tension was a bitch and she'd tightened every muscle during tonight's ordeal.

Once she'd seen Jared, felt his arm around her, and

known for certain he'd be okay, she had finally been able to breathe. She'd lay beside him as he slept, listening to the soft sounds of him snoring, so damned glad he was alive. And as she thanked God, Leo's words came back to her, reminding her of what was important.

She was finished being her own worst enemy. Finished running. And ready to tell Jared she loved him.

She also loved his family, who had been incredible earlier, bolstering her while she waited, trying to get her to go see him ahead of them. But Charlie thought his family should go first. Not to mention guilt kept her waiting until last.

Finally, Jared's dad had walked over and given her a lecture she'd wished her father had ever cared enough to give. "In this family, once you're in, you're in. Jared's feelings for you are obvious and that's enough for us. So stop tiptoeing around us and act like you belong. Because you do."

She did. She belonged with Jared.

She slept in his big bed, missing him, and the next morning, after a call from Alex, she arrived at the hospital bright and early.

If Jared was going home, she would be the one to take him.

THE DOCTOR ON shift signed Jared out of the hospital. The nurse took out his IV and gave him instructions not to get the staples wet for forty-eight hours. He listened to the instructions and said he'd make an appointment with his physician to have them removed in seven to ten days. A painkiller prescription was sent to his pharmacy but he didn't plan to take it. He'd deal with the pain using acetaminophen. No more falling asleep, waking up, and finding Charlotte gone.

"Do you have all that, Mr. Sterling?" the gray-haired nurse asked.

"He's got it. So do I," Charlotte said from where she'd been standing silently by the door.

He hadn't realized she was there, but damned if his mood didn't improve and his heart began beating stronger.

The nurse smiled at Charlotte, waving her in. "I was going to ask who was taking him home. Doctor's instructions. He's not to be alone for another forty-eight hours."

"I think we can handle that." She nodded, a surprising smile on her face. He wasn't sure what mood he'd get today, whether he'd have to track her down and talk her out of her guilt, or deconstruct her emotional walls.

So far, it seemed, he'd been wrong on all counts.

"Are you okay dressing?" the nurse asked.

"Yes." Nodding still wasn't a good idea.

"Then I'll leave you to it. Buzz when you're ready to leave. I'll call for a wheelchair." At his grimace, she said, "Hospital rules."

The nurse walked out and Charlotte walked in. Her cheeks were a healthy pink and her eyes bright. No sign of yesterday's guilt in sight. Trauma? Probably. He was still horrified by the possibility of her being hurt. She'd watched him get hit over the head with steel. Even he winced at that.

"Good morning," he said.

"Morning to you, too." He scanned her from head to toe, taking in the fitted shirt, highlighting the slight bump of her belly, and leggings.

A swell of pride and excitement filled him at the thought of seeing her getting large with his child. Because it was Charlotte he was having this baby with. He'd spent the morning making plans in his head. Plans he wasn't ready to share with her.

"You're here early," he noted.

She nodded. "Your father told me you were being released today, so I'm here to take you home."

He liked the take-charge tone she'd acquired between last night and this morning. "Then I should get dressed."

She strode to the closet in the corner of the room, opened the door, and pulled out a bag with his clothes, placing them on the bed. "I brought you a button-down shirt to wear so you don't need to try and pull something over your sore head."

He lifted his gaze. "Where did you sleep last night?" He'd assumed she went back to her apartment.

"Your bed." She dug into her large bag and pulled out one of his shirts, laying it on the hospital mattress. She leaned in close. "So I could smell your pillow all night."

He stared at her, stunned. "Who are you and what have you done with Charlotte?"

She leaned in and pressed her lips to his, then raised her head. "That was Charlie. Charlie was uncertain and afraid of her feelings and lacked the ability to trust. I'm Charlotte. And she almost lost you last night and all her insecurities became clear. And silly in light of life and death."

So that accounted for the change in her, making him wonder what else she had in store for him.

He called for the wheelchair and suffered the trip to the Uber downstairs. Together they rode in comfortable silence to his apartment building, him wincing at the potholes on the street. Once they arrived, they took the elevator to the penthouse.

"I know you must be in pain, and I swear this will only take a few minutes and I'll herd them back downstairs to Noah and Fallon at my place. But I couldn't talk them out of it," Charlotte said, just before the elevator doors opened.

"Welcome home, Daddy Jared!" the twins yelled with homemade welcome home signs in their hands.

They were a little loud for his concussed head, but he didn't care. Nor did he care that they still meant daddy in reference to his and Charlotte's baby. Over time he was going to let them find their own name for him. Knowing how he felt about Charlotte and all three girls, he absolutely knew what he wanted.

The twins? They were his and Charlotte's as much as they were Noah and Fallon's.

This woman wasn't going anywhere and he had a hunch she finally knew it.

Epilogue

TWO WEEKS LATER, staples out of Jared's head, life was looking up. The bastards who'd caused his injury had pleaded guilty, sparing him and Charlotte the ordeal of testifying at the trial. As for her brother, he'd turned on the other two and though he'd do time, it was everyone's hope, including Jared's, that he'd get clean. And this time stay that way.

Today, however, was a special day. Jared stood beside Charlotte as Dr. Messing, who they'd decided to use as her obstetrician, ran the wand over Charlotte's extended belly. There was a definite shift in her slender frame and the baby bump brought him sheer joy. He loved putting a hand over her stomach and though he hadn't felt the baby move, there were still a few more weeks for that, *she'd* felt internal flutters.

He was the typical first-time father, hovering, doting, and loving every minute. Jared had to limit his hours at the office due to the severe concussion and Brooke had taken over the brunt of the work. It wasn't fair but she was relying on another VP and swore things were running smoothly. Jared managed a few hours a day but he'd given in to the dizziness when it hit because the doctor said he'd heal faster if he did. Either way, he needed Aiden to get back to the States soon to help pick up the slack.

"Do you still want to know the sex?" Dr. Messing asked, bringing Jared's focus back to where it belonged.

"Yes," he and Charlotte said at the same time, and Jared held her hand tighter.

Chuckling, the doctor moved the wand around and paused. "And there *she* is." Dr. Messing went on to explain how they knew what they were looking at, but Jared had stopped listening at the word she.

"Another girl," Charlotte said, turning to face him. "We never talked about it. What did you want?"

"I—" He found it difficult to speak over the lump in his throat. "I wanted a healthy baby."

"And you have that," Dr. Messing said, stripping what looked like a condom off the wand.

Jared hadn't cared about the sex but now that he knew, he had visions of holding a tiny, bundled little girl in his arms. Taking her small hand and going places. And not letting any boys near her.

The doctor hit a button and a few seconds later, she handed Charlotte the printed photo.

"I'm going to leave you two alone. When you're ready, get dressed and meet me in my office and we can talk." With a smile, she strode out of the room.

"Oh my God," he said, once they were alone.

"What?" Charlotte asked.

"Three girls."

She laughed at what must be a panic-stricken look on his face. "I'll handle them just fine," she assured him.

She didn't get it. He wasn't talking about *her* three girls. It went deeper than that. During the last two weeks, when he'd been laid up, spending much of his time on Charlotte's couch once she returned home from work, Jared had gotten to know each of the twins and their individual personalities. He loved them.

"You don't have to handle it alone," he told her.

She nodded. "Oh, I know. I have Noah and Fallon with the twins and you with our girl. Who will need a name." She was smiling wide, her happiness evident, and he wanted her to always have that glow.

"No, I mean, you don't ever need to tackle life alone." He slid his hand into his pants pocket and pulled out the box he'd been carrying around since he'd felt steady enough on his feet to go ring shopping.

She gasped at the obvious-looking box. He'd been waiting for this exact day and time.

"Marry me, Charlotte, and we can raise this baby and the twins together."

Her mouth dropped open, her surprise clear. "What did you say?"

"Marry me and we can raise this baby and the twins together. Be a real family, though I have to tell you it already feels like we are one."

"Jared," she whispered as he popped open the box, revealing a three-carat round stone with two not-so-small pink sapphires on either side.

"A match to the necklace, except now we know the jeweler can add another pink sapphire to each. And every time we have another baby, we add another stone."

Her mouth parted and she was obviously speechless.

His heart skipped a beat. "I need a yes, Charlotte." Because there'd been a time he wasn't certain he'd get one. If he'd asked her at the wrong time, she'd assume the question was more about wanting her because of the baby than wanting her.

And then it dawned on him. He pulled the ring from the box, aware she was still in stunned silence. "I love you, Charlotte Kendall, and I want you to be my wife. Be by my side until death do us part."

"Yes." Her hand started to shake as he slipped on the ring. "I love you too." Tears flowed from her eyes, but he knew they were happy tears.

As happy as she made him, today and always.

★   ★   ★

CHARLOTTE, BECAUSE THAT'S how she thought of herself now, couldn't stop the tears any more than she could stop staring at the exquisite ring. She lay in the gown she'd changed into for the appointment and now had a huge ring on her finger.

"This is an engagement story our children will love." She held up the ring and the diamond sparkled in the sunlight streaming in from twelve floors above the street.

When she'd discovered she was pregnant while in Egypt, this happy ending was the last thing she'd expected.

He grinned. "I aim to please. Actually, I've been planning this since I fell asleep with you wrapped around me at the hospital. I thought it would be the perfect time."

"It is. But I really need to get dressed and we need to get to the doctor's office before they come banging on the door to see what we're doing in here."

He chuckled. "I wish. Before you get dressed, I have something I want to say."

She lifted her eyebrows. "What?"

"Thank you."

"For what?" she asked, utterly confused.

He rose to his feet. "For your trust. I know how

hard it was to give and I'll never do anything to make you regret it."

"I know," she whispered. Sitting up, she swung her legs over the side of the examination table.

The minute Jared went down from a tire iron, thanks to her brother, she realized all she had to lose. Almost losing him showed her how ridiculous her fears had been.

"You're my world, Jared. I adore you and I'll never lose faith in you or us again."

He pressed his mouth to hers and all was right in her world.

Epilogue 2

J ARED SAT IN the hospital room across from where Charlotte dozed in the bed. His shirt was unbuttoned and his baby girl lay on his bare chest, taking short little breaths. He adjusted the blanket over her back and took in all the good in his life. His daughter, Kylie Gigi Sterling, named after Charlotte's and Jared's mothers, with Gigi a more modernized version for Gloria Sterling. It was fitting, and when Charlotte suggested it, his heart filled… when he hadn't thought there was any more room.

They'd had a small wedding in his parents' yard because Charlotte wanted to be married before giving birth. Simple and sweet, the gown had draped around her large belly and she hadn't cared. She'd glowed with happiness as the twins walked down the aisle.

"Hi, Daddy." Charlotte's voice drew him out of his musings.

"I'm not sure I'll ever get used to hearing that."

Though Daddy Jared had stuck with the twins, especially after they'd gotten married, he loved it. They'd all moved into his larger penthouse and the girls had chosen their own rooms… with new paint colors. But they took turns sleeping in each other's queen-sized beds. Until they were older, this was what made them feel most secure.

"Sleep well?" he asked Charlotte.

"I was exhausted." But her smile was wide. "You and our daughter. It looks good on you," she murmured. He tucked the baby against his chest and rose to his feet.

He quietly made his way to the bed and once Charlotte had gotten into a comfortable position, he handed Kylie over.

Tears filled her eyes as she accepted the tiny bundle. "I never thought I could be this happy."

Leaning down, he pressed a kiss to her lips. "I love you and it will be my mission in life to keep you feeling this way."

"I love you too."

Smiling, he winked at her, then walked over to the bag he'd brought with him and pulled out a box with ROLEX stamped on the top.

She gasped. "What did you do?"

He grinned. "I'll open it for you so you don't have to give up the baby." He took a wooden box out of the paper one and opened it, revealing a yellow gold watch with a diamond bezel setting and diamonds for numbers on a pearl face.

Her eyes opened wide and she stared in awe. "It's

gorgeous," she said on a breathy whisper. "I've never dreamed of something like this."

"Sweetheart, it's nothing compared to what you've given me."

She had tears in her eyes, and he had a lump in his throat. Looking at her pale but happy and always beautiful face, he'd never been happier or more content, either.

"Wear it now," he said, clasping it onto her wrist, "and I'll bring it home when I leave so you don't have to worry about it in the hospital. You're being discharged tomorrow, right?"

She nodded.

"Good. I can't wait to bring my girls home." His cell buzzed and he glanced at the screen. "Speaking of girls, the twins are downstairs with my father and Lizzie. Ready for them to meet their sister?"

"I am."

"And I'm happy to have our family complete." He kissed her forehead and put away the boxes, then pulled out two pink T-shirts with BIG SISTER monogrammed on the front with silver sparkles. Next came a tiny onesie with BABY SISTER on the front.

"So adorable!" she exclaimed. "You've thought of everything. They're going to love them!"

"And I love them, Charlotte. Never doubt it. I utterly adore you." And he'd make sure she knew it every day for the rest of their lives.

Thanks for reading! Next up: Aiden Sterling and Brooke Snyder get their happily ever after!

Order and read
JUST ONE MORE TIME

JUST ONE MORE TIME

One night. One heartbreak. One man she could never forget.

Years ago, Brooke Snyder gave her heart—and her innocence—to Aiden Sterling, her best friend's older brother. For one perfect night, he was hers. Then he walked away without looking back.

Heartbroken, she focused on her career, and tried to move on, while he was half a world away. But no man ever measured up to Aiden, and the one time she tried, ended in disaster.

Now, he's back to help his ailing father, and avoiding him isn't an option—not when they're forced to work together and *definitely* not when she's sleeping in the bedroom next to his.

The past crackles between them, charged with everything they never said and everything they still feel. Every look dares her to remember. Every touch reminds her exactly what she spent years trying to forget.

Giving him her body is easy. But how can she protect her heart… when the man who broke it is the only one who can put it back together?

Order and read
JUST ONE MORE TIME

Want even more Carly books?

CARLY'S BOOKLIST by Series – visit:
https://www.carlyphillips.com/CPBooklist

Sign up for Carly's Newsletter:
https://www.carlyphillips.com/CPNewsletter

Join Carly's Corner on Facebook:
https://www.carlyphillips.com/CarlysCorner

Carly on Facebook:
https://www.carlyphillips.com/CPFanpage

Carly on Instagram:
https://www.carlyphillips.com/CPInstagram

Carly's Booklist

The Kingstons — newest series first

The Sterling Family
Book 1: Just One More Moment (Remington Sterling & Raven Walsh)

Book 2: Just One More Dare (Dex Kingston & Samantha Dare)

Book 3: Just One More Mistletoe (Max Corbin & Brandy Bloom)

Book 4: Just One More Temptation (Noah Powers & Fallon Sterling)

Book 5: Just One More Affair (Charlotte Kendall & Jared Sterling)

Book 6: Just One More Time (Brooke Snyder & Aiden Sterling)

The Kingston Family
Book 1: Just One Night (Linc Kingston & Jordan Greene)

Book 2: Just One Scandal (Chloe Kingston & Beck Daniels)

Book 3: Just One Chance (Xander Kingston & Sasha Keaton)

Book 4: Just One Spark (Dash Kingston & Cassidy Forrester)

Novella: Just Another Spark (Dash Kingston & Cassidy Forrester)
Book 5: Just One Wish (Axel Forrester)
Book 6: Just One Dare (Aurora Kingston & Nick Dare)
Book 7: Just One Kiss (Knox Sinclair & Jade Dare)
Book 8: Just One Taste (Asher Dare & Nicolette Bettencourt)
Book 9: Just One Fling (Harrison Dare & Winter Capwell)
Book 10: Just One Tease (Zach Dare & Hadley Stevens)
Book 10.5: Just One Summer (Maddox James & Gabriella Davenport)

The Dares — newest series first

Dare Nation
Book 1: Dare to Resist (Austin & Quinn)
Book 2: Dare to Tempt (Damon & Evie)
Book 3: Dare to Play (Jaxon & Macy)
Book 4: Dare to Stay (Brandon & Willow)
Novella: Dare to Tease (Hudson & Brianne)

* *Paul Dare's sperm donor kids*

The Sexy Series
Book 1: More Than Sexy (Jason Dare & Faith)
Book 2: Twice As Sexy (Tanner & Scarlett)
Book 3: Better Than Sexy (Landon & Vivienne)
Novella: Sexy Love (Shane & Amber)

The Knight Brothers
Book 1: Take Me Again (Sebastian & Ashley)
Book 2: Take Me Down (Parker & Emily)
Book 3: Dare Me Tonight (Ethan Knight & Sienna Dare)
Novella: Take The Bride (Sierra & Ryder)
Take Me Now – Short Story (Harper & Matt)

NY Dares Series (NY Dare Cousins)
Book 1: Dare to Surrender (Gabe & Isabelle)
Book 2: Dare to Submit (Decklan & Amanda)
Book 3: Dare to Seduce (Max & Lucy)

Dare to Love Series
Book 1: Dare to Love (Ian & Riley)
Book 2: Dare to Desire (Alex & Madison)
Book 3: Dare to Touch (Dylan & Olivia)
Book 4: Dare to Hold (Scott & Meg)
Book 5: Dare to Rock (Avery & Grey)
Book 6: Dare to Take (Tyler & Ella)
A Very Dare Christmas – Short Story (Ian & Riley)

** Sienna Dare gets together with Ethan Knight in **The Knight Brothers** (Dare Me Tonight).*

** Jason Dare gets together with Faith in the **Sexy Series** (More Than Sexy).*

For the most recent Carly books, visit CARLY'S BOOKLIST page
www.carlyphillips.com/CPBooklist

Other Indie Series — newest series first

Hot Heroes Series

Book 1: Touch You Now (Kane & Halley)

Book 2: Hold You Now (Jake & Phoebe)

Book 3: Need You Now (Braden & Juliette)

Book 4: Want You Now (Kyle & Andi)

Bodyguard Bad Boys

Book 1: Rock Me (Ben & Summer)

Book 2: Tempt Me (Austin & Mia)

Novella: His To Protect (Shane & Talia)

Billionaire Bad Boys

Book 1: Going Down Easy (Kaden & Lexie)

Book 2: Going Down Fast (Lucas & Maxie)

Book 3: Going Down Hard (Derek & Cassie)

Book 4: Going In Deep (Julian & Kendall)

Going Down Again – Short Story (Kaden & Lexie)

For the most recent Carly books, visit CARLY'S
BOOKLIST page

www.carlyphillips.com/CPBooklist

Carly's Originally Traditionally Published Books

Serendipity's Finest Series

Book 1: Perfect Fit (Mike & Cara)

Book 2: Perfect Fling (Cole & Erin)

Book 3: Perfect Together (Sam & Nicole)

Book 4: Perfect Strangers (Luke & Alexa)

Serendipity Series

Book 1: Serendipity (Ethan & Faith)

Book 2: Kismet (Trevor & Lissa)

Book 3: Destiny (Nash & Kelly)

Book 4: Fated (Nick & Kate)

Book 5: Karma (Dare & Liza)

Costas Sisters

Book 1: Under the Boardwalk (Quinn & Ariana)

Book 2: Summer of Love (Ryan & Zoe)

Ty and Hunter

Book 1: Cross My Heart (Ty & Lilly)

Book 2: Sealed with a Kiss (Hunter & Molly)

The Lucky Series

Book 1: Lucky Charm (Derek & Gabrielle)

Book 2: Lucky Streak (Mike & Amber)

Book 3: Lucky Break (Jason & Lauren)

The Most Eligible Bachelor Series
Book 1: Kiss Me if You Can (Sam & Lexie)
Book 2: Love Me If You Dare (Rafe & Sara)

The Hot Zone
Book 1: Hot Stuff (Brandon & Annabelle)
Book 2: Hot Number (Damian & Micki)
Book 3: Hot Item (Riley & Sophie)
Book 4: Hot Property (John & Amy)

The Chandler Brothers
Book 1: The Bachelor (Roman & Charlotte)
Book 2: The Playboy (Rick & Kendall)
Book 3: The Heartbreaker (Chase & Sloane)

The Simply Series
Book 1: Simply Sinful (Kane & Kayla)
Book 2: Simply Scandalous (Logan & Catherine)
Book 3: Simply Sensual (Ben & Gracie)
Book 4: Body Heat (Jake & Brianne)
Book 5: Simply Sexy (Colin & Rina)

Carly Classics
Book 1: The Right Choice (Mike & Carly)
Book 2: Perfect Partners (Griffin & Chelsie)
Book 3: Unexpected Chances (Dylan & Holly)
Book 4: Worthy of Love (Kevin & Nikki)

For the most recent Carly books, visit CARLY'S
BOOKLIST page
www.carlyphillips.com/CPBooklist

Carly's Still Traditionally Published Books

Stand-Alone Books

Brazen

Secret Fantasy

Seduce Me

The Seduction

More Than Words Volume 7 – Compassion Can't Wait

Naughty Under the Mistletoe

Grey's Anatomy 101 Essay

For the most recent Carly books, visit CARLY'S BOOKLIST page

www.carlyphillips.com/CPBooklist

About the Author

NY Times, Wall Street Journal, and USA Today Bestseller, Carly Phillips is the queen of Alpha Heroes, at least according to The Harlequin Junkie Reviewer. Carly married her college sweetheart and lives in Purchase, NY along with her crazy dogs who are featured on her Facebook and Instagram pages. The author of over 75 romance novels, she has raised two incredible daughters and is now an empty nester. Carly's book, The Bachelor, was chosen by Kelly Ripa as her first romance club pick. Carly loves social media and interacting with her readers. Want to keep up with Carly? Sign up for her newsletter and receive TWO FREE books at www.carlyphillips.com.